Don't miss these other books based on
Scooby-Doo 2: Monsters Unleashed:

Scooby-Doo 2 Book of Monsters:
The Official Movie Scrapbook

Scooby-Doo 2: Monsters Unleashed:
Joke Book

SCOOBY DOO 2 ™

MONSTERS UNLEASHED

WORLDWIDE PUBLISHING ™

SCHOLASTIC INC.

New York   Toronto   London   Auckland   Sydney
Mexico City   New Delhi   Hong Kong   Buenos Aires

No part of this publication may be reproduced in whole or in
part, or stored in a retrieval system, or transmitted in any
form or by any means, electronic, mechanical, photocopying,
recording, or otherwise, without written permission of the
publisher. For information regarding permission, write to
Scholastic Inc., Attention: Permissions Department,
557 Broadway, New York, NY 10012.
ISBN 0-439-56755-6
Copyright © 2004 by Hanna-Barbera.
SCOOBY-DOO and all related characters and
elements are trademarks of and © Hanna-Barbera.
Published by Scholastic Inc. All rights reserved.
(s04)
SCHOLASTIC and associated logos are trademarks
and/or registered trademarks of Scholastic Inc.
Designed by Louise Bova
12 11 10 9 8 7 6 5 4 3   4 5 6 7 8 9/0
Printed in the U.S.A.
First printing, March 2004

CHAPTER 1

VELMA

It was hard to believe, really — all of this, just for us! I squirmed uncomfortably in the back of the stretch Mystery Machine–style limousine and looked around at the other members of Mystery, Inc. Scooby and Shaggy were eating, as usual, popping burgers into their mouths and slurping down milk shakes. Fred was watching Daphne perfect her makeup. The two of them had just become engaged, and it had brought them closer than ever.

We were on our way to the grand opening of the Coolsonian Criminology Museum in our hometown, Coolsville, USA. We'd been invited as the guests of honor! It was certainly a special occasion, so I was all dressed up — and hating it! I have to admit, though, we all looked like stars in our fancy clothes. But I sure didn't feel like one. I just felt itchy in that poufy dress.

The limo slowed down in front of the museum. My heart started to race. I can't get used to the crazy crowds who've started turning out to see Mystery, Inc. A few years ago, we were just four teens and a dog who liked to solve weird mysteries. But our last case had brought us so much fame that we were suddenly celebrities.

The limo stopped, and our driver opened my door. "Ladies and gentlemen, we've arrived," he announced. We climbed out and were greeted by throngs of screaming, adoring fans. I looked over my shoulder at Shaggy and saw that he was so excited about the crowd that he didn't notice Scooby sneaking a sip of his milk shake — not even when the straw got stuck on Scooby's tongue and he accidentally whacked the limo driver in the face with the cup! Luckily, the driver didn't seem to mind.

Camera crews from all the national and local TV stations had sound and light equipment pointed at us. I had to squint my eyes. I probably looked like a total goofball. Reporters with microphones stood all along the red carpet leading to the entrance of the new museum.

A group of teenage boys yelled Daphne's name, holding up their shirts to show that her face was tattooed on their chests. Daphne smiled at them, but I could tell she thought the tattoos were just as creepy as I did.

Teenage girls screamed at the sight of Fred, and he loved it. He'd brought lots of extra ascots to pass out, and a few of the girls burst into tears at receiving a little piece of Fred.

A whole group of skaters shouted out to Shaggy, and a pack of dogs even surrounded Scooby! They'd brought dog bowls for him to sign.

"Velma! Velma! Velma!" Suddenly I realized there was a group of kids wearing T-shirts that said DINKLY BRIGADE on them, and they were chanting my name. I hadn't expected to have any fans here! I felt my cheeks get hot, and I snorted a little while signing autographs for them. Maybe this wasn't so bad after all.

A glamorous female reporter hurried over to us with a cameraman by her side. He was really hyper and kept darting in and out, trying to frame us between his fingers to test different camera angles. "May I have a word with Coolsville's hottest detectives?" the reporter asked.

Fred wiggled his eyebrows at her, trying to be Mr. Cool. "Absolutely," he said.

I hate it when Fred acts like that. Daphne hates it, too. Especially when there's a glamorous female at the receiving end. She covered it well, though, smiling sweetly at the reporter and saying, "Well, there you go, that's your word. C'mon, Fred — we're late!"

But suddenly floodlights were turned on, practically blinding us. "Heather Jasper-Howe, here at the grand opening of the Coolsonian Criminology Museum," the reporter said, facing the TV cameras. "I'm with the guests of honor, the master detectives of Mystery, Incorporated." She stepped closer to Fred, talking only to him. "With all your success, are you still going to have time for all of us here in li'l ol' Coolsville?"

"Of course, 'little old' Coolsville can solve its problems without us," he replied, trying to sound humble, "but we'll always be here to help. We love it here!"

The crowd cheered. Fred could be annoying at times, but he always knew the right thing to say. He was a real crowd-pleaser. He probably would have gone on talking much longer, but Heather Jasper-Howe seemed out of time. "Thanks, guys," she said. "I'm a huge fan. See you inside." She turned to the cameraman. "Come on, Ned, let's go."

We were stopped by several other reporters but, finally, we made our way inside the museum. "Jeepers," I murmured, totally impressed by the high ceiling and all the marble. It was *so* fancy! A quartet played classical music, and people in tuxedos and gowns chatted.

What really awed me, though, were the glass showcases that displayed some very familiar costumes. They were outfits worn by the various bad guys in the different cases we'd solved. Fred told me that we had donated them to the museum, but I hadn't ever actually seen all the costumes together in one place like this before. It was impressive.

We walked over to the display of a costume worn by a guy we called the 10,000 Volt Ghost. Instantly reporters surrounded us. "How do you feel right now?" a reporter called out.

"Mystery, Inc. is proud to donate the costumes of the criminals we've unmasked in the past," Fred replied.

"Those costumes include the 10,000 Volt Ghost here," Daphne added, "and the Black Knight Ghost, the freaky Skeleton Men, and even the dreaded Pterodactyl Ghost."

"We've also donated the costumes of some of our more ridiculous foes," I added, "like Chickenstein."

I pointed to the nearby case holding the Chickenstein costume. The crowd chuckled, but I noticed that Scooby and Shaggy weren't laughing.

They stood there, staring at the Chickenstein costume and trembling fearfully. "What's wrong?" I asked them.

"*Ridiculous?*" Shaggy asked in a shaky voice. "Obviously you forgot that dude tried to pluck us!"

Before I could reply, Daphne interjected, "Come on, guys, remember what I told you?" I had no idea what she was talking about.

Shaggy thought he knew, though. "Image is everything?" he asked, still quaking at the thought of Chickenstein.

"Yes. Image is everything," Daphne repeated. "And the whole city's watching — so let's keep a brave face."

Scooby and Shaggy could be such wimps! "Besides, there's nothing to be afraid of. They're just costumes," I assured them.

We walked over to a curtained glass case. "She's right," Shaggy said to Scooby, who was still shivering with fear. "Up close, they're totally fake."

"Totally," I assured Scooby as I yanked back the curtain covering the case and revealed the Pterodactyl Ghost inside. Though I'd scolded Shaggy and Scooby for being afraid, I had to admit that it looked eerily lifelike to me. It even sent a little chill of fear up *my* spine.

I pulled the curtain shut and hurried to find Daphne and Fred. They were just up ahead.

Fred was standing in front of a display on the Tar Monster, answering a reporter's question. "The Tar Monster scared locals away from the city of Byzantius in order to take their treasure. But, on the positive side, he'd pave your driveway for free! Right, Velma? Velmster?"

The reporters were cracking up, and now everyone had turned to look at me. Normally, I would have joined right in with the joke and given them more information about the Tar Monster. But at that moment I was completely distracted by an amazing sight!

Patrick Wisely, the brilliant curator of the museum, was walking straight toward me! He happened to be the most attractive guy I'd ever seen. It was as if — jinkies! — as if he was approaching in slow motion. I guess love is like that. Then, still in slo-mo, he slipped and fell flat on his face. He rolled to his feet in front of me. "Hey there," he said.

I was too dazzled to reply. Luckily, Daphne was right there. I turned to her. "Daphne, this is, uh, Patrick Wisely, the curator here."

Still feeling love-struck and shy, I managed to glance at Patrick. He smiled at me.

Daphne grinned at both of us. I think she could

tell love was in the air. "Well, Patrick," she said. "I hope you'll work closely with our Velma on the ever-expanding exhibit."

The group of reporters moved on and Daphne walked off along with it. That left Patrick and me alone, gazing at each other, face-to-face. Patrick spoke first. "Velma, listen . . . I know you're a glamorous, mysterious, jet-set adventurer who's preoccupied with international intrigue and all. . . ."

"Yes . . . uh . . . that's me," I said. It was so *not* me, but if that's what he thought, I wasn't going to disagree.

Our faces moved closer and closer together as he continued talking. ". . . But there's a symposium coming up on syntactic reasoning in the criminal brain and . . ."

Syntactic reasoning! The criminal mind! We were made for each other! We had the same interests, the same intellectual fascination with crime! "I've always found a criminal's incorrect use of the interrogative pronoun delightfully absurd," I told him.

"Me too," he said. "So, maybe you'd like to go together?"

I suddenly snapped out of the blissful love fog I'd been in. Was he asking me on a date? He was! But dates terrified me! I never knew how to act on a date — what to wear, what to say! "I ... uh ... don't have time," I stammered. "Mystery is my mistress. I must heed her sweet call."

Patrick looked so disappointed. I was angry at myself, but the date thing was just too scary. Not knowing what else to do, I hurried away and searched for the rest of the gang.

I spotted them standing together back where we'd first come in. The quartet's music rose over the sound of clinking glasses and polite chatter as I made my way through the crowd.

I had almost reached my friends when — in a blinding flash — a lightning bolt lit the sky outside the large museum window. It shattered the window, spraying glass everywhere! People screamed!

Reporters snapped pictures as a ghostly green smoke rushed into the room from outside.

CHAPTER 2

DAPHNE

I've worked really hard to shed my wimpy "damsel in distress" image. So when this weird smoke started rushing into the room, I was alert and ready to act. I noticed a display case nearby that had a curtain pulled shut around it. The curtain was now moving, as if some mysterious force was blowing inside it. The case began to glow from within and I ran over to yank aside the flapping curtain.

"Golly," I murmured.

It was the case that had displayed the costume for the Pterodactyl Ghost. Only now a living, humanoid Pterodactyl Ghost appeared inside! It flapped its huge wings and its eyes were sickly, bloodshot slits. The creature's scaly skin glowed with a green-and-yellow light. It screeched, and the earsplitting sound shattered the case, knocking me backward onto the floor.

The monster leaped out of the case onto the floor, crouching and looking around with a menacing glare. The crowd screamed and ran away.

"We need to make a plan," Fred shouted as people raced screaming out of the museum.

"This is *our* plan!" Shaggy said. He and Scooby began howling in fear.

"Stop!" Fred ordered them.

"In case you haven't noticed, Fred, there's a UFO in here," Shaggy said. "An unidentified freaky object!"

"Come on, you chickens!" Velma urged them. "Grab these ropes!" They helped her unhook some velvet ropes that had been used to mark off a display. But all three of them froze in fear when another case shattered.

The Pterodactyl Ghost had smashed open the case containing the costume once worn by the Black Knight Ghost. It had grabbed the costume with its beak and now stood staring angrily at Velma, Shaggy, and Scooby.

Fred put part two of our plan into action and yanked down the window's tall curtains. "We've got the curtains, Velma," he shouted as he tossed an end of the cloth to me. Together, we ran around the Pterodactyl Ghost, wrapping its body in curtains. It screeched and struggled to free itself.

I knew it would take more than this to hold the creature. "Shaggy," I shouted. "Use the rope to tie it up!"

Shaggy and Scooby ran around the Pterodactyl Ghost in opposite directions, each one of them holding an end of a velvet rope. "We tied it!" Shaggy shouted back to Fred and me. "You can let go of the curtains!"

We leaped back and let go of the curtains. The monster should've been tied with the velvet rope — but it wasn't. Instead, Scooby and Shaggy had accidentally tied *themselves* to the Pterodactyl Ghost! They looked at us with panic on their faces.

"Oops," Shaggy said.

The Pterodactyl Ghost screeched as it flapped its gigantic wings and rose into the air. Scooby and Shaggy were pulled onto their stomachs when the creature moved. As it flew around the room, it dragged them, screaming in terror, across the floor.

At that moment, an evil laugh filled the room. Everyone turned to the broken window, where the laughter had come from. Smoke surrounded a masked, caped figure that hovered in the night sky outside the broken window. A black hood covered his eyes, and a strange mechanical device was wrapped around his nose and mouth.

"Come, my pet," he called to the Pterodactyl Ghost. The device over his mouth must have been changing his voice, because he sounded like a robot. "Come, my pet," he repeated. "Bring me my prize!"

The Pterodactyl Ghost squawked and flapped its wings. It flew toward its master, pulling Shaggy and Scooby onto the banquet table. They grabbed pots and stuck them under their butts like sleds. That helped them surf over the hot serving dishes until the Pterodactyl Ghost flew even higher into the air.

"We have to save Shaggy and Scooby!" Fred yelled as the Pterodactyl Ghost pulled Scooby and Shaggy up with it. They dangled from the velvet ropes tied to its legs and smashed into one display case after another.

"As usual," Velma added.

The costumes in the cases toppled to the floor, crashing around us. The Pterodactyl Ghost grabbed the 10,000 Volt Ghost's costume just as I scooped up the sword that fell from the costume worn by Redbeard's Ghost.

The Pterodactyl Ghost headed out the window with Scooby and Shaggy, but I was determined not to let it take my pals. Using all my new martial arts skills, I lunged into the air in a crouching tiger position and — *swish, whoosh, slice* — I slashed at the velvet rope that tied them to its legs. Screaming, they tumbled onto the floor, falling into a pile of costumes.

The Evil Masked Figure let out another of his blood-chilling peals of laughter. "Citizens of Coolsville!" He spoke to the crowd in a booming, robotic voice. "This is only the first rung on the ladder of your demise!" The Evil Masked Figure turned a little so that he was staring right at me and the gang. "And this time, Mystery, Inc., you'll be the ones unmasked — as the buffoons you truly are!"

CHAPTER 3

FRED

What a mess! Broken glass, spilled food, and crumpled costumes were everywhere. The gang and I got right on the case, searching for clues to who was behind this disaster.

Velma examined the shattered display case that once held the Pterodactyl Ghost's costume. "Look! There's a secret trapdoor in this case!" she said. We gathered around her to get a better look at it. It was obviously how the live Pterodactyl Ghost had gotten into the case. Velma bent and lifted something small and shiny from near the door opening. She held it up on the tip of her finger. "A reptile scale!" she said. "A most wonderful clue."

This was truly a mysterious situation. "He stole two costumes — the Black Knight Ghost and the 10,000 Volt Ghost. Why?" I pondered out loud.

I wasn't the only one wondering, either. The entire crowd watched us as we tried to unravel the perplexing mystery.

Heather Jasper-Howe stepped forward and spoke into her microphone. "Fred and Daphne, could you answer a couple of questions for the press?"

Daphne stepped closer to me. "I don't know, Fred," she whispered. "We've always faced reporters *after* we've unmasked the creeps. We looked ridiculous back there."

"Don't worry," I assured her. "The press loves us."

Daphne smiled and nodded. She knew I was pretty good at dealing with reporters, so she walked up alongside me to talk to Heather Jasper-Howe.

The next morning, when I met the gang at our new headquarters in downtown Coolsville, I was feeling good. I thought Daphne and I had handled the press like pros. I couldn't wait to see the interview on the morning news.

We all gathered around the TV. Scenes from the night's events were already playing on the screen. Heather Jasper-Howe's voice spoke over the film footage. "It was utter disaster as two of the gang's key members are seen here causing untold damage to Coolsville's coolest new tourist attraction." The TV showed Scooby and Shaggy smashing into the costume displays.

I didn't think that was very fair! She didn't say that they were being dragged by a giant ptero-dactyl. It looked as if they were crashing into them on purpose.

"When asked to comment," Heather contin-ued, "Fred Jones, leader of Mystery, Inc., had this to say."

My face came on the screen. It was the inter-view I had filmed when I was on the red carpet. "'Little old' Coolsville can solve its problems without us," I was saying.

I clicked off the TV in disgust. "I didn't say that! I mean, I *did*, but that's out of context!" I shouted.

"It happens all the time," Velma commented glumly. "No matter what you said, it wouldn't have made a difference. Everyone blames us for what happened. People are canceling appoint-ments left and right. If we don't do something, we'll be Mystery, Blink."

"Over before we know it," Daphne added with a sigh.

"And it's all my fault." Velma sighed. "How many times do I have to learn? I'm the one who told Shaggy and Scooby to get the ropes."

Daphne chimed in, "It's *my* fault. I told Scooby and Shaggy to tie them."

The two of them looked so upset that I had to do something. It was time to take the lead and be strong for all of us. "No, it's *my* fault for not overruling you both. But it'll be all right — if we stay strong, in control, and work fast," I said firmly.

Velma nodded. "Let's get to the lab and figure a way out of this Jurassic jumble."

"That's the spirit," I said, trying to be encouraging. The three of us headed to our new high-tech crime-solving lab.

We didn't have much to go on, but the entire future of Mystery, Inc. was at stake. We had to solve this crime.

CHAPTER 4

SHAGGY

Fred, Daphne, and Velma disappeared into the lab, leaving Scoob and me behind. They didn't even notice that we weren't with them. Why should they? It wasn't like we had been much help. We'd never been much help to them. How had I not noticed before?

I turned to Scoob. "Face it, pal . . . we're screwups."

He nodded sadly.

"I mean, looking back, I guess every time they make a plan, we *do* mess it up somehow," I went on. "I just never really, like, noticed it before."

"Ree neither," Scooby agreed.

It was true. Last night had opened my eyes to the horrible fact that Scooby and I were *not* great detectives. My whole world was crumbling around me. "We must be, like, totally embarrassing to them."

Scooby nodded again. How could he, like, *not* agree with me? The truth had become so clear. But I wasn't about to give up so easily. Self-improvement was always possible, wasn't it? "There's got to be some way we can make everybody think we deserve to be in the gang, right?" I said.

Scooby sat up eagerly.

I was getting excited by the idea, too. "We have to act more like real detectives," I said. "You know, use our intelligent . . . ive . . . ness . . . icity." I stood and raised my right hand. "Scooby, raise your hand and repeat after me," I instructed. "From this day forward we will no longer be our goofy selves."

"Rah rara rah ra rah ar rahrahrah ar rah," Scooby repeated my words. In his own way, of course.

"We will be awesome detectives," I continued. "We will act just like the masters, Velma, Fred, and Daphne! We will be terrific, fantastic, and spectacular — and cease to be, uh, loser-rific, stink-tastic, and blah-tacular."

"Ra ra ra rahtacular," Scooby repeated.

I smiled, already feeling more detectivorial. Now all we had to do was *look* like detectives. The two of us had the same idea at the same time.

We ran around the office collecting pieces of clothing from the best detectives we knew — Fred, Daphne, and Velma.

In minutes, I had on Fred's ascot. Scooby was dressed in Velma's orange sweater and Daphne's white boots. "Let's go show the gang," I said.

Feeling good about ourselves, we burst into the crime lab and showed off our new detective-like appearances.

"What the heck are you guys doing?" Fred asked.

"Scooby, you're going to stretch out my sweater!" Velma scolded, hurrying toward us. "Yes, I have thirty-eight others just like it, but still. . . ."

"Like, Daphne said, 'Image is everything.' So we figured the first step to solving a crime is wearing the right attire," I explained.

"You're going to solve the mystery by dressing like us?" Daphne questioned.

"And by using the most important part of our bodies — our brains!" I added.

Ding! A scientific, crime-solving laser machine sounded. Scooby and I jumped to attention. We ran over to a slot where a piece of paper was sliding out.

"Ah! Clues!" I said, examining it. But though I tried, I couldn't tell what the squiggly lines on the paper meant. "What are these strange markings?" I asked.

Fred turned the paper right side up. "They're words," he informed me.

"Ah, yes, right," I said, feeling pretty foolish.

Velma plucked the paper from my hand and studied it. "Okay," she said after a moment. "Our test has come back positive. This is a real pterodactyl scale."

"Just as I suspected!" I said, even though I had no clue what was going on. "Daphne, explain it to the others."

"It means . . . the monster was real, and not a costume," Daphne explained.

"I'm still probing its chemical composition," Velma said. "The results will be ready in a couple of hours."

Clearly our attempts to be detectivorial were going unappreciated. The gang was whizzing ahead of us — as usual.

"Whoever did this seemed to have a need to take revenge on the city and humiliate us," Fred deduced.

"What if it's a guy we unmasked?" Daphne asked.

"But who would be able to create a *real* Ptero-dactyl Ghost?" Velma asked.

Daphne's eyes brightened with an idea. She pushed a button on the crime-solving computer. A picture of Dr. Jonathan Jacobo, the original Pterodactyl Ghost, filled a large screen on the wall. Seeing his tangled, bushy hair and creepy face again gave me the shivers.

"I remember that case like it was yesterday," Velma said. "Jacobo flew in a hang glider that he'd disguised as a pterodactyl. He robbed armored trucks carrying money and flew off with his loot. He planned to use the cash to pay for his eerie experiments. Jacobo was trying to create a monster army!"

"Until we captured him, of course," Fred added. He tapped his chin thoughtfully. "So you think Jacobo's behind this?"

"No," Velma disagreed. "He came to an unfortunate end during an attempted prison escape. He tried to fly away using a hang glider he built from prison bed frames and sheets. He got as far as the ocean surrounding the prison and then . . . down he went."

Daphne went to the computer and searched for any information on Jacobo. She clicked past old news stories and came to something more recent. "What about this?" she said as she quickly read the words on the screen. "Jacobo's cell mate was released from prison two months ago . . . Jeremiah Wickles!"

"Old Man Wickles!" I cried. Scooby and I started shaking. Old Man Wickles was a seriously sinister guy!

"The Black Knight Ghost!" Fred said excitedly. "That's one of the costumes that was stolen."

"Seems like he deserves a visit before any of our other creepy conquests make a comeback," Velma said.

Scooby and I sat down, feeling pretty disappointed in ourselves. Once again, the rest of the gang had figured everything out without our help.

And not only had they zoomed past us in brainpower, they'd zoomed past us in real life. While Scoob and I were feeling sorry for ourselves, they'd gone right out the door!

"Hey! Wait for us!" I yelled.

CHAPTER 5

DAPHNE

Fred parked the Mystery Machine at the curb in front of a run-down, eerie mansion. I cross-checked the address on my laptop computer. "Five-oh-five Troll Court. Old Man Wickles's ancestral manor."

"Oh, man," Shaggy whined, "another creepy crib! Why don't we ever have to investigate, like, a Burger King or something?"

"Stop complaining," Velma told him.

"Don't get me wrong," Shaggy declared. "I don't mind creepy stuff. Creepy is my middle name."

Scooby was trying to act tough, too, and growled like a junkyard dog. I wondered what had gotten into them.

"That's it, guys," Fred encouraged them. "A good detective should never betray that he experiences any of the weaker feelings."

Fred certainly was speaking from experience. He always remained calm and strong, no matter what. Sometimes I wondered if he ever wanted to let his guard down, but he never did.

"Weaker feelings?" Shaggy asked. "Like what?"

"Insecurity or fear," Fred answered. He acted like those were two things that never even occurred to him.

Shaggy, on the other hand, was a bit different. "Fear?! What about, like, *fright*?"

"That, too, sure," Fred answered.

Shaggy was getting more worked up by the minute. *"Terror?!"*

Fred nodded. He didn't bother to tell Shaggy that all of those were different words for the same thing.

And Shaggy was shocked! "No fear, fright, or terror?" he asked, staring at Fred like he couldn't believe what he was hearing. "The only feeling left is, like, hunger, man! Doesn't a detective get kinda lonely, all bottled up like that?"

As goofy as Shaggy was sometimes, he definitely had a point. It seemed like Fred was thinking about it for a minute, but his answer was as strong as ever. "No. I mean, he doesn't want anyone to think he's a wimp. Let's go."

We piled out of the van and passed a NO TRES-PASSING sign as we climbed up the cracked, moss-covered walkway. A kid on a bike zipped past us. "Great job last night, losers!" he called over his shoulder.

I felt my face burning with anger. I'd never been called a loser before. "Quick! We have to think of a comeback," I said. No one suggested anything, so it was up to me. "Hey, shut up!" I shouted. It wasn't the wittiest thing I'd ever said, but it was all I could think of at the moment.

We continued up to the front door. Fred pushed the doorbell. "You are trespassing on Wickles Manor," a loud voice boomed.

I thought that was pretty mean and I was getting tired of people being mean to us. "What kind of jerk makes that his doorbell?" I asked.

"He probably had too many magazine salesmen," Velma suggested.

Fred rang the bell again. "Leave now or pay the price," the voice threatened. "You have been warned."

Shaggy and Scooby dropped their tough-guy act and started shivering. "Man, it said we're going to pay a price," Shaggy whimpered.

"Shaggy," Fred scolded. "What could possibly happen by pushing a doorbell?" He pushed it again — and a trapdoor opened underneath our feet!

We were falling, plummeting down a metal

chute. It was full of twists and turns as it sped us around until, finally, we shot out at the bottom into a wire cage. With groans and shouts, we landed in a pile on top of one another. The cage moved against a wall and another one took its place, waiting for the next victim.

"*That's* what could happen by pressing a doorbell, Fred!" Shaggy yelled. "That!"

The sinister voice from the doorbell now spoke to us from a speaker on the wall. "At nine p.m. the owner will come home to set you free."

I looked around. There was a cute little Camper Scout who had come to the door selling cookies. Two salesmen were also trapped in another cage.

I heard Velma sigh and turned to see what she was thinking. "Just great," she said. "The lock's on a laser thumbprint scanner."

That meant that only Old Man Wickles's thumbprint could undo the lock. I suddenly had an idea. "I need my makeup kit," I said.

"Daph, now?" Velma questioned.

I grinned at her. I know she doesn't care about girly things like makeup, but this time I had more than glamour in mind. I wasn't going to tell her that, though. I'd let her be surprised — and impressed. "It's never too late to learn to apply makeup properly," I said mysteriously.

I took my makeup bag from my purse. With it

in my hand, I crawled over to the thumbprint scanner. "Let's see," I said. "The last authorized thumbprint will still be here."

Blush powder was what I needed next. I brushed it on the print and — as I'd hoped — the thumbprint showed right up. The next step was to lift the print off the scanner. I didn't have tape, but I had something just as good — pore cleanser strips. I pressed one on Old Man Wickles's print and the print came up onto the pore strip.

All that was left to do was to put the pore strip on my thumb, press the scanner, and — *bing* — the cage door slid open.

The gang stared at me with awestruck respect. It was just the effect I'd hoped for. But I simply shrugged modestly. "I enjoy being a girl."

The gang and I quickly set the two salesmen and the Camper Scout free. They darted out the door, though Shaggy managed to buy a box of cookies before the Camper Scout left. Then we carefully made our way upstairs.

The first room we came to was an old, dusty library. "Hey, look! Shiny footprints," I said, pointing to the glowing marks on the floor. "What do you think somebody stepped in?"

"Maybe Scooby's been eating glow sticks again," Fred suggested.

We followed the prints deeper into the library. The shelves were lined with books about the supernatural. Fred pulled one from the shelf. "It looks as if he's been reading this one recently," he said, opening it. "It's not dusty like the others. But I can't read this writing."

Velma came alongside him and looked at the pages. "It's an ancient Celtic text used by secret societies in the mid-nineteenth century. The title is, roughly, *How to Make a Monster.*"

We all exchanged meaningful glances. Making monsters was exactly what someone had done the other night at the Coolsonian Criminology Museum. I looked over Velma's shoulder as she turned to the front page. It contained a list of all the people who had owned the book through the ages. The most recent name on the list was J. Jacobo!

"This belonged to the original Pterodactyl Ghost!" I cried.

"Maybe he gave it to Wickles before he died," Fred suggested.

Velma began thumbing through the pages, reading quickly. "It's a combination of science and magic," she told us. "There's a list of ingredients for creating your own carbon-based organic-composite predators. In other words . . ."

"Monsters!" Fred, Velma, and I said at the same time.

Suddenly I noticed that Shaggy and Scooby hadn't come into the library with us. We all turned to look for them, but they weren't there.

"I hope Shaggy and Scooby are finding equally intriguing clues," Fred said.

CHAPTER 6

SHAGGY

When the gang had turned left, Scoob and I went right, searching for clues on our own in creepy Wickles Manor. We were in a dark hallway when I held a magnifying glass to my eye and discovered something amazing. "Whoa! Everything's, like, totally bigger when you look through this thing."

Scooby gave me a thumbs-up. He appreciated a good discovery when he heard it. I inspected him with the magnifier and learned something else that shocked me. "You totally have fleas, Scooby." I examined myself next. "I totally have fleas, too!"

We both felt the intense need to scratch. So we did.

But then it was time to get serious. "All right, Scoob," I said. "Let's split up to double our chances."

Scooby grabbed hold of me and whimpered. I

almost started whimpering, too. Then I remembered our promise — to act more like real detectives. "Come on, bro," I said to Scoob. "We've gotta be fearless, like Fred said, right?"

Scooby nodded, even though he was still holding on to me.

"I'll meet you back here," I added as I pried him off of me.

I hurried off down the hall using my magnifying glass to search for clues. To tell the truth, it was making me kind of dizzy. I put it in my back pocket as I entered a gloomy old room. Old Man Wickles sure had an eerie-looking place. Just standing there in that room was scaring me.

Suddenly I whirled around toward the door. Someone was coming in!

It was Scooby, and he was dressed in boxer shorts, a wizard's hat, and sunglasses. His arms were full of things that he dumped onto the floor in front of me. "Rues!" he said proudly.

"Scooby, those aren't *clues*. They're just things you want." I pointed to a toilet brush he'd brought in. "Like, why is that a clue?"

Scooby picked up the toilet brush and sang into it as if it were a microphone. "Rooby-dooby-doo!"

"Just 'cause you can sing into it doesn't make it a clue!" I told him. "It just makes it *awesome*!"

Then I noticed something that might actually *be* a clue. A yellow Post-it was stuck onto Scooby's foot. I lifted it off and read it aloud. It said: TODAY — 5:30. THE FAUX GHOST.

This was a real breakthrough. "Dude! We *are* detectives!" I cried. "You found a clue! The Faux Ghost is a hangout for bad guys. Now what do we do with this clue?"

"Re can rolve re rystery," Scooby said.

"Bro! Are you kidding?" I asked. I didn't think we were smart enough to solve a case all on our own. I supposed we could try, but I was afraid we'd mess things up.

Suddenly we heard something creaking toward us. A creepy cackle echoed in the room. And then he appeared from out of nowhere!

"Like, the Black Knight Ghost!" I cried.

He was right there in the room with us. Old Man Wickles had once dressed up as the Black Knight Ghost, but this armor-covered creep looked very real to me. It was horrible!

Scoob and I weren't sure what brave and fearless detectives should do. So we did what we always do — we screamed and ran!

We sped down the hall and darted into a room filled with suits of armor. We quickly slammed the door shut behind us. Thinking fast, we piled the armor against the door. "Let's see him get through this," I said as we continued piling furniture and everything else in the room on top of the armor.

We were a great team. Scooby handed things to me and I put them on the pile. I was working so fast that I didn't even stop to look at him. I just had to reach out and he placed something in my hand. "Thanks," I said as he handed me a piece of armor.

"You're welcome," he replied. Only, it wasn't Scooby's voice. In fact, I suddenly noticed that Scooby was piling things up on the other side of me.

If he was *there,* and I was *here,* then who else was in the room with us? Slowly, I turned . . . and faced the Black Knight Ghost!

Scooby saw him at the same time that I did. We howled in fear as the huge knight lifted us up and hurled us into our pile of stuff. The whole mountain of things we'd stacked against the door crashed under us.

We lay there in a heap. We couldn't get up, couldn't even move. All we could do was lie there and quake with, like, total terror as the Black Knight Ghost drew his sword.

CHAPTER 7

VELMA

We heard Shaggy and Scooby screaming and ran toward them, following the sound. When we got to the room where the screams came from, we burst in, jumping over furniture and armor that lay scattered on the floor.

I could hardly believe my eyes. The Black Knight Ghost had come to life! Just the other evening it had been no more than a costume at the exhibit. Now he was here — and he was about to behead Shaggy and Scooby!

Fred picked up a sword and shield from a suit of armor and held it in front of him. "Yo, metalhead!" he shouted at the Black Knight Ghost.

The Black Knight Ghost forgot about Scooby and Shaggy and started toward Fred. He held his own sword and shield high. Fred wasn't scared, though. "Bring it," he said defiantly.

The ghost whacked Fred hard with his shield. *Clang!*

"He brought it," Fred moaned as he fell to the floor, unconscious.

Once again, the Black Knight Ghost raised his sword high, preparing to slice off Fred's head. But when he brought it down toward Fred's neck, it clanged against a knight's lance. It was held by Daphne. She'd grabbed it from the pile of things on the floor.

Daphne jumped up and faced the Black Knight Ghost. She's become a master swordswoman, but the Black Knight Ghost was awfully good, too.

Daphne was fighting hard, but I didn't know how long she could hold him off. I figured that the only way I could help was by using my brain.

I still clutched the book of ancient magic we'd found. Maybe it contained some formula or something that would stop the Black Knight Ghost. I began flipping though the pages and soon came across a very complicated-looking math formula. Luckily, I'm sort of a mathematical genius. This was one whomping formula, though, and it took a lot of figuring out. I wasn't even finished with it when the lance flew out of Daphne's hand and the Black Knight Ghost hurled her across the room.

I kept reading as he turned toward me, raising his sword and preparing to strike. I figured out the formula just in time. Basically, it boiled down to this advice — kick him and run. Thanks to the formula, my kick was well placed. "Mommy," the ghost whimpered in pain.

"Nighty-night, knight," I told him. "Now run!" I yelled to the rest of the gang.

We all charged out of the room and headed straight out the front door. We piled into the van and Fred hit the gas. My heart didn't stop pounding until we were back in our office with the door safely locked.

"Like, guys, Scooby's feeling kinda under the weather," Shaggy announced. It was true — Scooby looked horrible! He was foaming at the mouth and moaning. "He needs some, like, fresh air," Shaggy continued. "We'll catch up with you later."

We watched the two of them leave, and Fred looked at Daphne and me, worried. "That's the third time this month he's gotten rabies," he said. But we knew that if anyone could help Scooby, Shaggy could. So it was time to get back to business. Maybe our research would make more sense now that we had the ancient book from Wickles Manor.

I went to the crime lab and pulled up the computer files that held our research. Feeling hopeful, I opened the file that had the results of the computer scan I'd run on the reptile scale. "Jinkies," I murmured as I read.

"What is it, Velm?" Fred asked, coming up alongside me.

I walked back to the outside office and opened the book of ancient magic. It was just as I'd thought. "Our analysis of the pterodactyl scale shows that it contains randamonium, which this book says is *the* critical ingredient needed to make a monster."

Daphne joined us, looking over our shoulders at the book. "Doesn't randamonium glow?" she asked. "Remember those footprints in the library?"

She was right! This was definitely another important clue. "If we can prove Wickles is behind this, Coolsville will dig us more than ever!" Fred said.

"Where would Wickles get randamonium?" Daphne wondered.

"Randamonium is a by-product of certain silver mines," I recalled.

"Like the ones at the abandoned mining town in Old Coolsville," Fred suggested.

"We should . . ." I'd had an idea, but it flew right out of my mind. That was because I was completely distracted by something totally unexpected I'd spotted through our front window. Patrick, the director of the Coolsonian Criminology Museum — the man of my dreams — was about to ring our front doorbell!

The doorbell rang. I dove behind our couch. The bell rang again as I crawled quickly toward the crime lab. Although I was hopelessly in love with Patrick, I couldn't face the idea of going on a date. As adorable as he was, dates terrified me.

"Keep him here," Daphne told Fred.

I crawled even faster toward the crime lab. It was the best hiding spot I could think of.

"What are you doing?" Daphne asked as she got onto her hands and knees and crawled alongside me.

"He wants to ask me on a . . . a . . . date!" I explained, feeling panic-stricken.

"It's okay to be scared," Daphne said.

"I'm not scared," I argued. "I've fought werewolves and ghosts but I know that, at the end, we always unmask them and it's just little, scared men inside. No, I'm much more comfortable with the world of logic and facts. And I'm not . . . hot."

"Me neither," said Daphne sadly. "When I look in the mirror, all I see are my hideous earlobes." Then she perked up again. "But that's why God made long hair and earrings! Everyone has flaws, Velma. The object of a healthy relationship is to never let the other person know they're there."

I sighed. "I really like this guy. What would you do if someone thought you were some glamorous and mysterious jet-setter?"

"I'd make myself one," Daphne declared. "Follow me."

Together we crawled into the crime lab. Daphne found her emergency makeup bag, her hair stuff, and her secret stash of clothing. She quickly got to work on my makeover.

Outside, I could hear Patrick talking to Fred. Would this work? Could Daphne's flair for style turn even a hopeless case like me into a glamorous person of mystery?

"Perfect," Daphne declared when she was done. "You can wear this." She pulled a tight-fitting leather outfit from her bag. "Come on," she urged me. "You'll look great in it."

I didn't think so, but Daphne was the expert. "Okay," I agreed and squirmed into it. I was too nervous to even look in the mirror.

"All you have to do now is act the part," Daphne instructed me. "Act like a jet-set adventurer. Believe it!"

Tossing my head back bravely, I walked into the front office where Fred and Patrick were still talking. Patrick's eyes widened when he saw me. He was clearly stunned by my new look. "Velma?" he asked.

I opened my mouth to say something, but no sound came out. Daphne jumped in to help me. "Sorry we're late," she said to Patrick. "Velma was just showing me some new, exotic fighting moves she learned on her latest trip to Togo. Show Patrick, Velma."

Togo? I'd never been to Togo! Then I got it. Daphne was trying to make me look like an exotic woman of mystery to impress Patrick.

I gave it my best try, swinging my arms and kicking while I shouted martial arts kinds of cries.

"I wouldn't want to come up against that in a deadly battle," Fred said. The gang was really trying to help me.

"Absolutely," Daphne agreed.

"Gosh! Wow!" Patrick said. "I've always wanted to be a detective like you guys. Only, I'm not in a gang. Well, I was . . . in tech school. We were the crip . . . tologists."

"Guys, we have a mystery to solve," Fred said. I could see he was eager to get on with the case.

Patrick realized it, too. He faced me and started talking a mile a minute. "Anyway, I came here because I was just . . . I was thinking about what you said yesterday, Velma, about how you didn't have time to go out. And I thought, *What the heck, why don't I help her work on the case? That way we could hang out and solve the mystery.*"

"We're professionals, Patrick," Fred said. "We don't give tours of —"

"But we *can* give rides," Daphne interrupted him. "We can give you a ride to the museum, which is right on the way."

I didn't know whether to be angry at Daphne or to thank her. But, either way, I wound up sitting in the backseat of the Mystery Machine next to Patrick.

"You know, Velma, I have to admit that you're a little . . . different . . . than I thought. I mean, you're as . . . beautiful as ever, but I'm not sure a guy like me would fit into your world," he stuttered.

For the first time, I looked in the rearview mirror and saw how Daphne had made me over. Wow! Did I ever look changed! No wonder Patrick thought I was different! I was about to explain to him that this wasn't the real me, but something stopped me. Maybe it was the look of total horror he now wore on his face.

I followed his gaze, and my jaw dropped. "Jinkies," I murmured.

CHAPTER 8

DAPHNE

We all stared out at the front of the Coolsonian Criminology Museum. It was obvious that *something* awful had just happened. Police cars were parked everywhere. Museum guards wandered on the sidewalk looking dazed and confused. Reporters and camera people poured out of news vans and, all around, people gawked at the scene.

"My museum!" Patrick cried.

I'd tried hard to light the fire in Velma's romance with Patrick, but this latest disaster had really thrown a bucket of cold water on the flames of love. He climbed out of the van and ran up the museum steps without even a glance back at Velma.

We climbed out of the van and that news viper, Heather Jasper-Howe, was right there, sticking a microphone in Fred's face. Her crazy cameraman, Ned, was darting around looking for the best camera angle, as usual.

"Any comments on the museum robbery?" Heather asked Fred.

Fred was pretty stunned by the scene, but he did his best to answer. "We're investigating the two stolen costumes as we speak," he said.

"No, I mean the robbery that *just* happened," she explained. "The one where the Black Knight Ghost and the 10,000 Volt Ghost stole the *rest* of the costumes."

"The rest of the costumes?" Fred cried. Then he forced himself to calm down. "I mean, yes, yes. We know exactly what's happened because Mystery, Inc. is always in control."

"So what you're saying is that it's all downhill for Mystery, Inc.?" Heather Jasper-Howe asked sweetly. I could tell that she was trying to make a fool out of Fred — for the second time!

"Yes. No. Hey!" Fred said, completely confused. "You're doing that thing again where you'll take everything I say out of context! You're trying to get me to say Coolsville stinks again so . . . No! Don't record that."

"Let's go inside," I suggested to Velma. I couldn't stand there and watch that horrible woman make Fred say whatever she wanted him to say. Velma and I hurried up the steps and into the museum.

When we walked into the main lobby, Patrick

stood looking at his broken, destroyed exhibit. Every single costume had been taken. There was even more shattered glass on the floor than there had been the night before.

Velma walked up behind Patrick and put her hand on his shoulder. "Patrick, I'm sorry," she said. "This must be so hard for you."

"I just . . ." he began, but then his voice became rough and he seemed to choke up. "I'm sorry. I have to go." He stumbled toward the door.

"Go where?" she called after him.

"I don't know. I have to figure out what's going on here," he replied.

Together we watched him run out of the museum. "He's using all this as an excuse to get as far away from me as he can," Velma said sadly. "I should have known. A cool guy like him could never go for me."

I sighed. Why couldn't Velma see that Patrick was crazy about her? Velma unzipped the leather outfit I had lent her. Underneath she still had on her sweater, skirt, and knee socks. She wiped the makeup off her face. So much for the *new* Velma.

Fred ran in, carrying a newspaper. Our picture was on the front page! Then I saw the headline above it: MYSTERY STINK!

I could feel myself turning red with anger. Velma just shook her head sadly.

I have to give Fred credit for staying calm. "Come on, gang," he said. "Let's go to the mining town. We have a mystery to solve."

He was setting a good example, but it wasn't easy — especially when we got into the Mystery Machine and turned on the radio. The first thing we heard was Heather Jasper-Howe's voice reporting the news. ". . . all Fred Jones said was, 'Coolsville stinks.'"

Once again she'd taken his words and twisted them around. Fred just closed his eyes — and then slammed his head on the dashboard.

That was it! I couldn't stand what Heather Jasper-Howe was doing to Fred and the rest of us. I spotted her at the side of the museum finishing her broadcast. "I'll be right back," I said, slipping out of the van.

I ran back to the museum and hurried up the steps to confront Heather and her hyper cameraman. "What's up with the personal attacks?" I asked her angrily.

The sweet smile she always wore faded from her face. "Don't act tough with me," she came back forcefully. "I know what you're about. You think you can dazzle everyone with your pearly whites. But what do you do for the gang, really? Velma is the smart one. Fred's the leader. All you are is the pretty face. Everyone knows there's nothing on the inside."

I was stunned. "Why are you doing this?" I asked.

"Because it's my job to unmask those who pretend to be who they're not," she replied.

Unmask? Where had I heard that word recently? The evil hooded figure from the night before! "You sound like . . ." Then I paused. It was a wild idea, too wild. But still . . .

"You sound just like the evil masked guy! But you know that, don't you? Because just as you know I'm standing here, you know that I know you know who you know you are, which is him, who's a her, which is you!" I was on to her!

Heather looked amused. "Oh, now I see what you do for the gang. You're in charge of incoherent babbling."

I was about to say something witty back to her, but I was distracted by an all-too-familiar evil cackle of laughter. Looking up sharply, I saw the Evil Masked Figure standing on the roof of the museum.

"Citizens of Coolsville," he called. "Once again your city and your heroes have proven useless before my power. Enjoy your last days of freedom — soon Coolsville will be *mine*!"

Heather scrambled to get her microphone. But the masked man spread his cape wide and disappeared.

"Darn it!" Heather Jasper-Howe shouted. Then she turned on me. "You made me miss the biggest news scoop yet! Can't you do anything right?"

I didn't care about her scoop, but I'd missed a chance to get closer to the Evil Masked Figure. And I'd been wrong about Heather being him. How could she be, when I'd just seen both of them at the same time? I'd even let Patrick run away without getting him together with Velma!

Maybe Heather was right. Maybe I was just all looks and no brains.

CHAPTER 9

SHAGGY

I felt bad lying to the gang about Scooby feeling sick, but it was the only way we could sneak away and prove ourselves as mondo-groovy detectives. Plus, after we escaped from that scary Black Knight Ghost, the day, like, totally improved. For one thing, Scoob and I found a diner with an all-you-can-eat food bar. By the time we finished eating all we could, the sun was setting.

I belched and turned to Scooby. "I guess we should get back to solving this case," I said. "Let's go to the Faux Ghost."

He burped and nodded. We left the diner and headed to the Faux Ghost, a seedy nightspot where many lowlife, bad-guy types hang out. "We can hide behind this trash Dumpster and see who goes in," I suggested. Scoob agreed.

It didn't take long for the shady, sinister, and no-good to start showing up.

A big tough guy smoking a cigar was the first one I recognized. "Remember him? That's C. L. Magnus," I whispered to Scooby, who crouched beside me behind the big trash container. "He used to dress up as Redbeard's Ghost."

The next one to go in was a woman some might say was attractive — if they liked evil, scary women, that is. "Do you remember her? That's Aggie Wilkins," I told Scoob. "She was also known as the Ozark Witch. These are all, like, folks we unmasked, man! If they spot us, they'll invite us to a weenie roast — one where we're the weenies!"

Scooby pointed across the street. He'd spotted a store with lots of underworld-style clothing in the window.

"Groovy, Scooby!" I said. "Detectives *do* go undercover, don't they?" We crept out from behind the Dumpster and scurried over to the shop to buy our tough-guy outfits.

In less than ten minutes we were outfitted and looking *bad* — not the good bad, the really bad bad. Scooby had on a wig, star-shaped sunglasses, a bright jumpsuit, and platform tennis shoes that lit up when he walked. I had found a purple suit and hat that made me look *mean*.

When we walked through the crowd in that club, heads turned. "Hey, hey, hey," I said in my coolest bad-guy voice. "Everybody part like the

Red Sea! It's me, Shizzy McCreepy and my brother, S. D. McCrawley — in the house and ready to parh-tay!"

The no-good customers stared at us as we bopped and strutted our stuff. The place was like a criminal clubhouse, full of banners and posters of Coolsville's most famous (and most evil) villains. Aggie Wilkins sidled up to Scooby and looked him over. "Hello, handsome," she cooed.

"Rel-lo," Scooby replied smoothly. But before he could say anything else, a giant, tattooed tough guy pushed her aside and grabbed Scoob by the collar.

"This is a private club," he growled. "The only way you can belong is by dressing up as a terrifying creature and scaring the crud out of innocent people."

I rushed to Scooby's side and spoke to the giant goon who was threatening him. "I guess you don't know that my brother and me are the famous West Coast Pickleaculas — fifty percent pickle, fifty percent Dracula, one hundred percent terrifying!"

I gave him my scariest look and the dude stepped back, impressed. "Cool!" he said. "I was the Cotton Candy Glob."

We had definitely fooled this guy, which was a good thing because I could tell that the real

Shaggy and Scooby would have been pretty un-popular in this club. For one thing, off to the side was a boxing gym and the speed bags everyone was punching were decorated with some familiar faces — Fred's, Velma's, Daphne's, Scooby's, and mine! Zoinks! And the gopher-pounding game had been changed into a Mystery, Inc.–pounding game. It made my head hurt just to watch it.

I was so busy looking around and absorbing all the bad vibes that I didn't notice that a fight had broken out. One of the fighters was thrown right into Scooby. He would have flattened Scoob if someone hadn't pulled my pal out of the way just in time.

"Watch it, idiots!" the amazingly ugly old dude who had just saved Scooby shouted.

My jaw dropped when I realized who he was. "Old Man Wickles!" I gasped.

He glared at me. "Leave me alone," he said, walking away.

I couldn't let him get away. He was one of our main suspects! "Your portrayal of the Black Knight Ghost was like a, uh, inspiration to my brother and me," I gushed. I figured that everyone likes to be flattered. He might stick around if I praised him. "It's because of you that we decided to dress up like a couple of weird and

They're back! Fred, Daphne, Velma, Shaggy, and Scooby-Doo are investigating a brand-new case — and it's their spookiest yet!

Mystery, Inc. is the hottest thing in Coolsville!

Mystery fans galore show their support for Shaggy, Velma, Daphne, and Fred.

Zoinks! Like, all the monsters the gang has ever faced are out to get them!

So Shaggy and Scooby decide to go undercover as bad guys at an all-monster nightclub.

The gang investigates a creepy old mansion ... then regroups in their high school clubhouse.

The whole gang bravely faces down the monsters. Another mystery solved!

evil Pickleaculas. Have you done anything, like, really cool and evil lately?"

The old guy stared at us suspiciously, but I suspected that I was winning him over. "Listen," he croaked. "I ain't usually for the giving of advice, but I feel sorry for you due to your brother's hideous deformity."

Aw, poor Scooby! He touched his nose self-consciously.

"Get out of the game while you got the chance," Wickles went on. "We ain't nothing to be admired. We coulda done something good with our lives, but instead we dressed up like supernatural idiots 'cause we wanted people to think we was magical and important and powerful. Why? Because that was the opposite of what we really felt."

I was really touched by his, like, heartfelt words. "Wow!" I said. "I guess you're sorta, like, grateful to Mystery, Inc. for unmasking you, huh?"

Wickles reached into a bowl and scooped out a handful of peanuts. Then he laid them on the table and banged them under his withered old fist. "Are you kidding?" he shouted. "If I saw those twerps I'd pound them like these nuts!" He continued to smash the peanuts until they were just dust under his fingers.

It was just a little, like, upsetting. "Uh . . . I

think I hear the Cotton Candy Glob calling us," I said nervously.

"Rye-rye," Scooby said, waving to Wickles.

We hurried away from the creepy old dude. I wanted to get out of there as fast as we could, but nature called and I had to make a trip to the bathroom.

"Don't do anything to attract attention," I told Scooby when I left him. But by the time I came out, I found Scooby leading a dance line. All the creepy thugs in the place were following him as he boogied around the dance floor. When he saw me, he whirled around and waved. That's when his wig went flying across the room.

The dancers stopped dancing.

The band stopped playing.

Everyone froze except for Scooby. He kept dancing and smiling. But then, slowly, he realized that everyone was staring at him.

"That's Scooby-Doo!" C. L. Magnus, the guy with the cigar, shouted. "He's the meddling mutt that helped throw us in jail!"

Scooby started to shake and shiver. I ran in front of him. "No, man, this is S. D. McCrawley," I told the crowd. "He's just wearing a mask! See?" I grabbed Scooby's face and stretched it wide, letting it snap back into place. As I did this, though, my hat fell off.

"And you're 'Doo's best pal, Shaggy Rogers," the tattooed, former Cotton Candy Glob cried. The crowd began rumbling angrily.

"Zoinks!" I shouted as I warmed up my legs, getting ready to run. "Like, gangway!"

Scooby and I leaped over a table and into a trash chute. *Whoosh!* Down we slid and landed with a thud right inside a trash container. *Wham!* A load of garbage poured right down on top of us!

I smelled some tasty food in the garbage, but it was still pretty gross. It took us a few minutes before we could poke our heads out from under it all. When I did manage to see over the top of the container, I noticed two men talking in the shadows of a streetlight. One of them was the tattooed Cotton Candy Glob. The other guy was yelling at him. "Then find out," he shouted. "I want answers!"

The tattooed guy nodded and hurried off. The one who'd been yelling at him turned and began to walk toward us. I ducked lower in the container. When he stepped directly under the light I could see his face. It was Patrick!

He saw me at the same time I realized who he was. "Shaggy?" he called. "Scooby? What are you two doing here?"

"Uh . . . being undercover and stuff," I answered. "And you?"

"My museum was broken into again," he replied. "I came down here to see what I could find out. I had to put on that tough-guy act so these guys didn't eat me alive, you know?"

Like, I really didn't know. But I nodded anyway. I guess Patrick could tell I was faking it, because he got totally creepy all of a sudden. *"What?! You don't believe me?"* he screeched, his voice all spooky.

I looked at Scoob, and all we could do was gulp. What now?

But suddenly Patrick was back to his old self again. He laughed and punched me on the arm, like we were old pals. "Just kidding you, man! Sorry — it's hard not to, 'cause you're just so easy to scare."

He was right about that, but it was still weird. And then he got all freaky again! *". . . As you should be!"*

I felt my eyes get wide, but before I could run, normal Patrick was back again. "I'm joking, Shaggy! Chill out!" And then crazy Patrick jumped in again. *"NO! Do not chill out!"*

Zoinks! Scooby and I were ready to get out of there, but Patrick was laughing so hard that it seemed like the whole thing really was a joke.

"Sorry, sorry!" he said, catching his breath between laughs. "I gotta stop — man, I'm just a bit nervous, you know, with all this excitement."

Whatever. I spotted Old Man Wickles leaving the club by a side door. Scooby saw him, too. It was time to get away from the creepy curator. "Patrick, we could totally do this all night — and something tells me we would — but we gotta make like your personality and split." We took off, darting from building to building in the dark streets so Old Man Wickles wouldn't spot us.

Wickles stopped at a corner to wait for a traffic light. He turned and almost saw us. Scoob and I ducked behind a building just in time.

"I know what to do," I told Scooby. "We should split up so we're not so easy to spot." I'd come equipped for something like this. Reaching into my jacket pocket I pulled out two tin cans attached with a long string. "A phone," I explained to Scooby. "We talk through the cans. You take one can and I'll take the other. This way we can stay in touch with each other while we follow Wickles."

The light changed and Wickles crossed the street. We hurried after him but went in different ways, stretching the string out between us as we went. "Scooby-Doo, can you hear me?" I whispered into my can.

"Rello," he replied.

It was working! We kept following Wickles through Coolsville. I soon realized where we were headed — and I didn't like it! "This is the oldest part of the city," I told Scooby, speaking into my can. "It's been deserted for a hundred years."

"Rolloooooo, Raggy!" he shouted into the phone.

"Yes, hello," I said. Scooby thought the phone was a toy and he was enjoying it just a little *too* much. "Now pay attention! The point is that Wickles has led us, like, into a terrifying ghost town!"

That made him get serious! "Roast rown?" he asked nervously.

"Yes," I replied. Suddenly my eardrums were nearly blown out by the sound of Scoob's terrified scream coming over the can phone! I hurried over to him to find out what was wrong. It was nothing major. The mining town was awfully dark and scary, and it had frightened him.

Unfortunately, Wickles heard the screaming and turned. I clapped a hand over Scooby's mouth and dragged him into an abandoned building.

Scooby stopped screaming and I let go of his snout. We peeked out the door as Wickles looked around.

I guess he thought the scream had been his imagination because, after a minute, he moved on into one of the creepy old buildings.

I looked over at Scoob, who was holding the tin can up to his eye now and trying to see through it. It was pretty funny, but if we were going to be, like, real detectives, we had to follow Wickles.

"Let's check it out," I suggested. Scooby and I clung to each other as we searched around in the dark old building, which turned out to be some abandoned silver plant. My teeth were chattering, and Scoob's paws were shaking like crazy!

At one point, Scooby got superspooked and jumped up into my arms. It was so dark, and we were so freaked out that it was hard to tell what happened next. All I knew was that I saw someone next to me that *wasn't* Scoob — and it only had one eye!

"Dude, did you see that?!" I asked Scooby, panicked. "It was, like, a guy with an eyeball for a head!"

Maybe I'd just been seeing things, though, because Scoob looked totally calm and shook his head no.

Hmm. I thought about it for a minute, then said, "Maybe it was, like, a reflection of your eye in a thing!" I chuckled in relief, and Scooby giggled, too. Guess a dark old building can make your imagination go a little crazy. Especially when you know there are monsters on the loose.

Just then, I realized that I had a book of matches in my pocket, so I pulled one out and lit it — anything would be better than just the little moonlight coming in from those spiderwebby windows. As it flared up, though, there was that huge eyeball again! Like, right in front of us — it was the Skeleton Man, one of the evil dudes we'd caught a long time ago!

How had Scoob not seen him? I glanced over at my pal and saw that he was crying. "Ri ras lying!" he whimpered.

We both screamed as the match went out. It was totally dark.

Scooby and I ran off, to who knows where — we couldn't see a thing! Next thing I knew, though, I tripped over something on the ground and went flying, and Scoob tripped over *me*. He must have fallen into some kind of lever, because the wall in front of us slid open. In the moonlight, I saw that there was an old elevator behind the wall.

"A definite clue," I said to Scooby. We looked at each other with frightened expressions. I could hear Scooby's teeth chattering. But we had promised to be brave detectives — so we forced ourselves to step into the elevator.

CHAPTER 10

FRED

I drove the Mystery Machine into the abandoned mining town in Old Coolsville. Daphne, Velma, and I got out and looked around at the empty run-down wooden buildings.

"Velmster, what's your assessment?" I asked. I could always count on Velma to give a level-headed, sensible evaluation of the situation.

"Love stinks," she grumbled.

That Patrick guy had really gotten to her! "I mean, regarding the monster situation," I explained.

"Oh. Yes." She shook her head and seemed to go back to her old unemotional, logical self. "This is a mining town where the Evil Masked Figure could have gotten the randamonium."

"Fred, do you think I'm just a pretty face?" Daphne asked me. I looked at her strangely.

What was she talking about? And why wasn't her mind on the case?

She looked up at me with wide, serious eyes, waiting for my reply so I had to say *something*. But what? How do you answer a question like that? "No . . . I mean, yes . . . I mean, not *fat*. Is that what you're looking for?"

"I just thought I figured out earlier who that evil masked freak might be," she explained. "But then . . . well, it sort of became clear that I was wrong and — fat? Why would you even say 'fat'?"

At that moment, we heard voices coming from a nearby building. We hurried over and peered in the window.

"Guys, I don't mean to ruin these tender moments. But monsters are trying to kill us." I whispered to Velma and Daphne. Inside, Old Man Wickles sat at a table laying out his evil plans to two men who were obviously his henchmen. This case was as good as solved. We had him now! The old coot was *so* busted!

There was no sense in waiting. I stepped up to the door and pushed it open. Velma and Daphne ran up behind me.

Old Man Wickles and his helpers stared at us in total shock.

"Old Man Wickles!" I cried. "We've caught you

red-handed in your foul, monster-making scheme with your ugly, evil henchmen."

One of the henchmen looked really insulted. "We're investors!" he cried. "We're here listening to Mr. Wickles's sales pitch."

I saw that they were sitting around a small-scale model in the middle of the table. It showed the mining town changed into an amusement theme park. A sign on the table read: YE OLDE TYME MYNING TOWNE AMUSEMENT PARK.

Oops. I could feel my face getting red with embarrassment.

Wickles shot me an irritated look and then went back to speaking to his investors. "So . . . as I was saying, Ye Olde Tyme Myning Towne will be a summer camp where kids can have a real old-fashioned mining experience. We'll send the little tykes deep into the mines with a pick and shovel, where they can dig for eighteen hours straight, just like in the golden days of yore. They'll have the time of their lives and we'll get free miners."

"Listen, Mr. Wickles," Velma interrupted. "We need to ask you a few questions about your ties to the recent monster attacks."

The investors looked to Wickles, interested in his response. I was pretty eager to hear what he had to say, too.

"I don't know nothing about no monsters!" Wickles snapped.

"Well, then why was there randamonium on the floor in your mansion?" Velma asked.

Wickles spread his arms wide. "There's randamonium all over this place!"

Looking down, we could see that there were glowing footprints everywhere.

He had an explanation for the randamonium, but I didn't want to let him off the hook too easily. "Are you continuing the work of your old pal Jonathan Jacobo?" I asked, getting right to the point.

"Old pal? Jacobo?" Wickles cried. "We hated each other!"

"Then why did we find that monster book in your library?" Velma questioned.

"Having a book doesn't make me responsible for anything!" he shouted. Then his eyes narrowed angrily and he stood. "Wait a second! You're the runts who vandalized my home! I'll call the cops on you, you diabolical little troublemakers! Which one of you stole my toilet brush?"

Before we could apologize or explain our actions, the two investors picked up their briefcases and stood. "I'm sorry, Jeremiah," one of them said to Wickles. "A scandal like this could hurt our image."

"Wait, fellas!" Wickles called after them. But they marched out the door without so much as a look back.

Wickles's face turned bright red with anger. He spun around to face us. "Why??!!" he exploded. "Wasn't it bad enough for you meddling teenyboppers to toss me into the pokey? Now you have to follow me around and ruin my life? This property is all I've got left after you brats took everything else from me!"

I never thought I'd find myself feeling sorry for Old Man Wickles, but the old guy's words affected me. Up till now I had always been certain that we were being helpful. Suddenly I wasn't so sure that we really knew what was right.

"Come on, gang," I said.

"What should we do now?" Daphne asked.

I shrugged, not really sure.

"Maybe we should look around," Velma suggested.

Wow! I was so shook up by Old Man Wickles that I forgot to suggest splitting up and looking for clues, the way I usually do. The old coot had really shaken me up!

CHAPTER 11

SHAGGY

The spooky old elevator started to move down. Scoob and I clung to each other, shaking and shivering. It kept going until it brought us down to an old laboratory full of weird tubes and beakers.

We stepped out of the elevator and saw the glowing randamonium that Fred had told us about speckled around the place. "Like, clue-topia," I said. We'd hit the clue jackpot!

We went in opposite directions to search every inch of the lab. The first thing I discovered was a massive metal door. On it was odd writing, just like the ancient writing in the *How to Make a Monster* book the gang had found in Old Man Wickles's library. I yanked hard on the door handle, but it wouldn't budge.

Looking over my shoulder, I saw Scooby open a big metal refrigerator. Inside were beakers full of colorful chemicals and bowls of something gloppy and glowing. Scooby dipped his paw in and scooped up the stuff, licking it. "Rogurt," he said.

The next interesting thing I discovered was some pretty complicated video equipment. A camera on a tripod was aimed at a green wall and a video monitor was mounted on another wall beside it. I stood in front of the green wall and waved at the camera. My face appeared on the monitor, but instead of there being a green wall behind me, it looked like I was standing in front of the Great Wall of China. "Look, Scoob, I'm in China!" I said, waving.

I pushed a button and the monitor still showed my face, but now I seemed to be in front of the Eiffel Tower in Paris, France. Strange!

Scooby didn't say anything in reply, so I looked over to see what he was doing.

"Zoinks!" I cried.

Instead of Scooby, I saw a freakishly bizarre monster standing right where Scooby had been just a minute ago! I screamed, and the monster looked over his shoulder. "Raggy?" he asked.

"Scooby? Dude! You turned into . . . Yao Ming!" I said. Scoob looked at himself in the shiny surface of a metal table. Then *he* started screaming.

I suddenly figured out what had happened.

That glowing stuff that he'd eaten had turned him into something else. "Oh, man, there's got to be, like, an antidote around here somewhere," I said.

Frantic to help my pal, I started pushing aside beakers and test tubes. Some green liquid spilled on my hand. "Oh, crud!" I cried. I was shaking all over. When I stopped, I thought I hadn't changed at all. But then I looked down and realized — I was a *girl*! "Aaah! I've got a chick's body!"

Scooby still looked like some crazy dog-version of Yao Ming.

I had to do something. Fast. I kept searching through all the scientific stuff on the table. I found some bottles that were marked with an A on their labels. "Maybe A stands for antidote," I said to Scooby. "Let's try it out." We each took a beaker marked A and drank from it.

By the time Scooby was done drinking, he'd grown a huge brain out of the top of his head. The good news was, I wasn't a chick anymore. The bad news was, I'd become extremely muscular, a regular Mr. America.

"Ah, knowledge, you hideous plague," Scooby said. But his words sounded like they should have come from someone brainy. "How I long for my blissful days of ignorance. Alas, perhaps I can brew some chemical concoction that will restore me to the simple, delighted creature I once was." He turned back to the chemicals and began mixing a little of this and a little of that.

Scooby wasn't the only one undergoing a brain change. "Yeah! I'm buff!" I shouted. My mind as well as my body had become supermacho. I felt out-of-control strong. "Check out my pecs, little man!" I boasted to Scooby as I flexed my arm muscles. I flexed until my veins bulged and my head felt ready to explode.

"Be still, oaf," Scooby scolded me as he mixed chemicals.

Even though I wasn't a supergenius like Scooby, I knew he was trying to change us back to our old selves — our old dumb, puny selves. "No way, brainiac!" I yelled, snatching a beaker out of his hand. "I'm gonna stay this way forever!" I tossed the beaker toward the huge door.

"Noooo!" Scooby yelled.

Too late! *Kaboom!*

The beaker exploded in a giant black cloud as it hit the door. The sound of our coughing filled the room. But when Scoob and I stopped, we heard other hacking coughs in the room. In another few minutes the smoke cleared and we saw Velma, Daphne, and Fred just outside the elevator. "This dithering buffoon practically killed us," Scooby explained to them.

"Go boom," I said, stunned by the explosion.

Scooby held out a beaker full of chemicals to me. When I didn't take it, he grabbed my head and poured it down. Then he gulped down the remainder. More shaking — and then we were back to ourselves.

"Whoa!" I said, holding my head.

"What the heck?" Fred asked.

"Ri inrented a rotion," Scooby told him proudly.

Fred looked at Daphne. "What?" he asked, confused.

"He invented a potion," she explained. "But what are you guys doing here? Scooby, you're supposed to be sick!" Daphne didn't look too happy with us.

Neither did Fred. "You guys lied to us! We're a team! You don't just go off half-cocked, doing whatever you want!"

Zoinks! Looks like our detectivorial attempts totally weren't appreciated by the rest of the gang. "Sorry, man," I apologized. "We were just trying to be really cool detectives, like you guys. . . ."

I didn't get to say any more, though, because Velma called to us — and she sounded like she'd found something important.

"Guys?" She was standing by a huge hole where the metal door had been before I blew it off. The door lay in pieces at her feet. We gathered around as she translated the ancient language of the door's strange inscription. "'Beware who enter the monster hive. Inside, your fears come alive.'"

We stepped through the hole into a room full of monster costumes! Every disguise that had been stolen from the museum hung inside clear pods mounted on the walls. There was also a big machine of some kind in the room.

"This must be where the Evil Masked Figure turned the Black Knight Ghost and the 10,000 Volt Ghost costumes into real monsters," Daphne said.

"They're all here," Fred observed. "Every costume from every villain we've unmasked."

Velma attempted to figure out what it all meant. "So, he turned the costumes into real monsters, which implies . . ."

". . . that he needs the costumes to make the monsters . . ." Fred finished, ". . . which implies . . ."

". . . that Patrick is the one. He's the bad guy," Velma concluded sadly. "That's why he wanted to go out with me — to get information."

"Maybe that *and* the fact that you're super-duper terrific," Daphne suggested. She was trying to make Velma feel better, but it didn't work.

"Patrick's the only one who had access to the Pterodactyl Ghost costume!" Velma explained. "And he left suddenly when we got to the museum."

"Yeah!" I cried. "We saw him hanging out at the criminals' lair."

Fred walked over to the big, strange-looking machine. "We need to shut this machine down for good — before *whoever* turns all the costumes into monsters."

Daphne ran her hand along an opening in the side of the machine. "Are the controls back there?" she wondered, moving into the space behind the machine. Fred and Velma followed her, leaving Scooby and me all alone.

We looked at each other and both of us started to tremble at the same time. But then I got myself under control. "Dude!" I said to Scooby. "We've got to get back to acting like mondo-groovy detectives and search for clues."

It took Scooby a little while longer to get his shaking and quivering under control, but pretty soon he was ready to go. We crept along the wall, searching for clues. It was pretty dark, so I flipped a switch, hoping to turn the lights on.

A light went on, all right. In fact, lots of lights lit up as the machine turned on. "Cool!" I said.
Thud!

Something fell on the floor and we turned to see what it was. One of the glass pods had opened and a criminal's costume belonging to the Miner 49er now lay on the floor, covered in some kind of glop.

This was terrible! "We've got to get him to go back!" I said. I pushed more buttons, hoping I'd find one that would put him back. But instead, more pods opened!

The Ozark Witch fell out, and then the Ghost Clown came down. Scooby began to whine. I wanted to scream for help, but I forced myself to remain calm. There had to be an OFF switch somewhere, right? I just had to find it. That's what Fred, Velma, and Daphne would do.

Even though Scooby was still crying and whimpering, he pointed to a large switch. "Good eye, Scoob," I praised him. "That's got to be it! Here we go!" I ran over and pulled the switch.

Dozens of pods began opening! It was horrible!

The Witch Doctor, Redbeard's Ghost, Captain Cutler's Ghost, and the Zombie all fell out of their pods. I was so horrified by what I'd done that I screamed — only no sound came out. That's how terrified I was.

Fred, Velma, and Daphne returned from be-hind the machine. "Well, we didn't find anything. . . ." Fred was saying, but he trailed off when he got a look at Miner 49er, who was now lifting his pickax scarifyingly over his head.

"Ya want this easy or hard? Take your *pick*!" he shouted. Cackling at his own joke, he swung the pick. All of us ran out of his way, screaming.

"Disconnect the control panel!" Velma shouted. "It'll stop the pods from opening!"

Fred nodded and headed for the panel. He had to hurl monsters out of his path to get there. The control panel was sort of like a Frisbee. He grabbed hold and yanked it off its base.

The pods stopped opening.

Dozens of monsters were free now — and it was all me and Scooby's fault. Fred had stopped hundreds more from being released — he'd bailed us out again. But there was no time to think about that.

"We've got to get out of here!" Fred shouted.

"Bring the control panel," Velma told him as we raced for the elevator. We jumped in just as the door was closing.

When we got up to the top, I breathed a sigh of relief. It didn't last long, though. Horrible creatures jumped out at us from behind the old, rusted machinery. They were skeletons with one large eyeball where their heads should have been! The eyeballs blinked at us and the Skeleton Men made squeaky, chittering sounds.

"Oh, man," I cried. "Like the old saying goes: Out of the frying pan and into the freaky skeleton dudes with eyeballs for heads!"

The Skeleton Men were bad enough, but then the 10,000 Volt Ghost climbed up out of the elevator shaft. It lunged at Fred, Velma, and Daphne. They ran and it chased after them. Scoob and I dashed off in another direction. The Skeleton Men were right behind us.

We raced out of the plant onto the moonlit streets of the old mining town. The Skeleton Men reached out and nearly grabbed us. We ran through the streets, but they stayed with us until we came out onto a dusty, steep hill.

Two trash cans nearby gave me an idea. I grabbed the lids and handed one to Scooby. We stood on them and pushed off, skidding down the hill.

Ha! I thought. We'd given those bony bums the slip. There was no way they could catch us.

Then I looked over my shoulder and saw that the Skeleton Men were using their own bones as skis and ski poles! Yikes! Whenever they fell, they were able to put themselves back together again and keep coming!

The slope divided into two paths. I took one

path and Scooby went down the other. The Skeleton Men split up, some of them chasing Scoob and some chasing me. Soon Scooby appeared again — and he was heading straight into me.

Bam!

We crashed and the next thing I knew, Scooby and I were flying off the edge of a cliff!

CHAPTER 12

VELMA

Daphne slid the mattress into place and Fred opened the side door of the Mystery Machine. *Bang! Thud!* Scooby and Shaggy flew in.

I wiped my forehead with relief. It had worked!

We had ditched the 10,000 Volt Ghost by jumping into the van and driving off at top speed. We were at the bottom of the cliff when I'd spotted Scooby and Shaggy flying off the end. I'd quickly calculated the rate of speed and angle of their fall and put this plan into action. "You guys okay?" I asked.

"Sure," Shaggy answered, rubbing his head, "as long as you define 'okay' as 'in massive agony.'"

Fred hopped back into the driver's seat. "Let's get to headquarters," he suggested as he started the engine.

"That'll be the first place the monsters will look for us," Daphne disagreed.

She was right, but I had another idea. "I think I know where to go," I said. Fred hit the gas and we sped off.

As the mining town disappeared behind us, Daphne turned on the TV we'd installed in the van. The scene we saw on the screen was unbelievable.

The monsters that had gotten free from their pods now roamed the streets of Coolsville, causing mayhem. A huge ghost ship, like the one Redbeard's Ghost had once used, sailed through the center of town with Redbeard's Ghost and Captain Cutler's Ghost at the helm. Chickenstein, the Zombie, and the Headless Horseman were there, along with dozens of others.

The Evil Masked Figure appeared and spoke to the camera. "Citizens, turn in Mystery, Inc. Your reward? We'll let you live!" He laughed hideously, then turned to his monsters. "Go! Find them!" he commanded.

One of my *least* favorite people appeared on the screen. "The situation is dire," Heather Jasper-Howe reported. "A monster army is turning Coolsville upside down in search of Mystery, Inc."

Fred slowed the Mystery Machine as we passed by our office. An angry crowd had gathered there. They held signs that said: UNMASK YOURSELVES. "Mystery Stink! Mystery Stink!" they chanted, but they ran away screaming when monsters poured into the street and began ripping apart our headquarters.

It was awful! But it could have been worse. "If this is what happens when *dozens* of monsters are loose, imagine what will happen if he lets all of them go," I said.

I glanced at Scooby and Shaggy and saw they had tears in their eyes. Obviously they felt responsible for all this, ashamed of the mistakes they'd made.

Heather Jasper-Howe came back on the TV. She was now in her news studio, although she was still disheveled and dirty from being out on the streets of Coolsville. "The Evil Masked Figure has sent in this tape," she told the television audience.

The Evil Masked Figure appeared on the TV screen again. "Coolsvillians, mark my words — unless Mystery, Inc. turn themselves over to me, my monster army will destroy your city and everything you hold dear. You do the math: *Your heroes are zeroes!*"

Heather Jasper-Howe returned to the screen. "I beg you, Mystery, Inc., if you can hear me, turn yourselves in!"

We watched, devastated. Was this all really our fault? Maybe turning ourselves in *was* the right thing to do.

"But if we do, he'll get the control panel back," Fred said, as if he'd heard my thoughts, "and the city will be in even worse shape."

"We'd be playing right into his hands," Daphne agreed.

As Heather Jasper-Howe continued to implore us to come in, the Black Knight Ghost smashed through the news studio door and the screen turned to buzzing white static.

"Come on, Fred," I said. "Let's go to our old high school clubhouse. We'll be safe there."

He nodded and headed in that direction. When we got there, I made sure to lug the big Frisbee-shaped control panel out with me. I was walking away toward the clubhouse when I realized Fred was still sitting inside the van. He looked completely stunned by everything we'd just been through.

Daphne walked back to the driver's side window. "Freddy, are you okay?" she asked. "Do you need to talk?"

His eyes still looked glazed over with shock. "Talking is for wimps," he said.

She helped him out of the van. As we all walked, I heard Shaggy talking to Scooby. "The

Evil Masked Figure's turning Coolsville into Ghoulsville and the gang's taking the hit for it," he said sadly. "This is the most our-faultest screwup ever."

Inside the old clubhouse, I was all flooded with memories of our high school days. We'd been so young, so eager, so full of hope. Back then, we solved mysteries for the love of them, not to prove anything to anybody. The mysteries seemed to unravel themselves. Sometimes the answers would just appear like magic.

The place was littered with old, out-of-date equipment. Wandering around, I picked up a small gray device that had been repaired with duct tape. "Jeepers!" I cried softly, recognizing it. "My first multiple resonance imaging device, made from a crystal radio and old video games." Seeing the imaging device made me suddenly think of something. "Randamonium has an algo-rhythmic cross-currency of negative four point one-two-one. With it, maybe we can —"

"— reverse the current!" Fred finished my thought. "That would reverse the monster-making process! It's genius!"

My heart pounded excitedly. "All we have to do is rewire the control panel. We bring it back to the monster hive . . ."

". . . and plug it back into the base," Daphne

joined in, "and all the monsters throughout the city will be destroyed!"

My mind was working hard now. "I'll need something to melt metal," I told them.

Fred grabbed his old toolbox from underneath a pile of junk. It'd just been gathering dust since he was small. The words LI'L TOUGH GUY were painted on the lid.

"L'il Tough Guy," Daphne read fondly. "I remember that."

Fred took out a tiny hammer and screwdriver. "Of course, I changed it a little," he said as he pulled a huge propane tank out of it. He rigged up the tank, turning it into a blowtorch. A flame shot across the room. It would certainly melt metal.

"I'll also need a soft, conductive, metal-like gold," I said.

Daphne slid the engagement ring Fred had given her from her finger. "Will this do?" she asked me.

"Babe, are you sure?" Fred said.

Daphne nodded. She was a little hesitant, but willing to sacrifice for the cause. Moments later, she'd removed three other rings, seven earrings, two necklaces, thirteen bracelets, six anklets, three toe rings, and a gold hair clip. "When the going gets tough," she declared, "the tough de-accessorize."

We finally had everything I needed. Without wasting a second, the three of us got to work. I opened *How to Make a Monster* and started my calculations. Daphne took apart a cordless phone, a Walkman, and an old computer to use for electronic parts. Fred used his blowtorch to melt down the jewelry.

It was just like old times: Mystery, Inc. was on the case!

CHAPTER 13

FRED

I heard screaming from outside the clubhouse and looked up from my blowtorch. Through the window, I saw Scooby and Shaggy running away, yelling. Captain Cutler's Ghost, the spook who wore a diving outfit and carried a speargun, had emerged from the nearby swamp.

"They've found us," I told Daphne and Velma. "You'll have to finish what you're doing in the van."

Daphne and Velma gathered up their equipment and the three of us piled into the Mystery Machine. I sped around the corner of the clubhouse to pick up Shaggy and Scooby. Captain Cutler's Ghost was aiming at them with his speargun as they ran for their lives!

Scoob and Shaggy raced into the van just in the nick of time, but Captain Cutler's Ghost managed to hook the back of the Mystery Machine with his spear. I floored the gas pedal, but the wheels only spun in place. Slowly but surely, the monster began pulling the van back to him.

I shifted the van into reverse. "Fine," I said defiantly. "If we can't go forward, let's go . . . back!"

The Mystery Machine zoomed backward and ran right into the salty devil, sending him splashing back into the swamp.

I kicked the van into gear and headed back toward Coolsville.

"Man! This day is tied for the most terrifying day of my life!" Shaggy said.

"Tied with what other day?" Velma asked.

"Every other day of my life!" Shaggy whined.

Velma crawled to the back of the van and looked out the window. "Jinkies!" she gasped.

I glanced over my shoulder and saw what had alarmed her. The Pterodactyl Ghost was flying right behind us! "Shaggy, take the wheel," I shouted, leaping to the back of the van. I found my blowtorch and pushed open the Mystery Machine's back door. "Take this!" I shouted as I aimed the blowtorch right at the Pterodactyl Ghost and prepared to fire.

The giant bird monster swung its big claw and he took it, all right — it snatched the blowtorch right out of my hand! "I didn't mean literally *take it*!" I cried.

"That was freaky," Shaggy said from behind me. Velma and Daphne were back there, too.

"Shaggy? Who's driving?" I asked nervously.

"Uh," Shaggy said as we all looked to the front of the van. No one was driving!

At that moment, the Pterodactyl Ghost reached in and yanked the van's shag carpeting right out from under us. Daphne and I were pulled along with it! We struggled to hold on as the carpet was dragged along behind the speeding, swerving van. The Pterodactyl Ghost also managed to pull Velma and Shaggy out of the Mystery Machine, and they clung desperately to the open, swinging doors.

As the van turned, I saw that we were headed straight for a huge gas tanker. If we hit it, the tanker would explode.

"Scooby! Turn the wheel!" Velma shouted.

Scooby pointed to the steering wheel, a confused expression on his face.

"Yes, that wheel!" she yelled.

Scooby was nervous and turned the wheel just slightly. It was enough, though. We avoided hitting the tanker by inches. But, just then, the Zombie jumped onto the windshield. Scooby was so surprised that he clutched the wheel and the Mystery Machine swerved madly all over the road.

The Pterodactyl Ghost was snapping at us with its huge jaws, but somehow Velma managed to pull herself back up into the van. She gave us all a hand back in — just in time.

I climbed up into the driver's seat and swerved around the Zombie, who had fallen off the van. Scooby's terrible driving had shaken it loose. And now we were heading straight into a big sign that stood on the side of the highway. The Pterodactyl Ghost was right on our trail.

I zoomed *under* the sign.

The Pterodactyl Ghost flew *into* it — and its beak got stuck there!

The van skidded to a halt in front of some old buildings just beyond the sign. Old cars and motorcycles were everywhere! We staggered out of the Mystery Machine. Velma climbed into the back of the van and came out again holding the control panel.

Looking around, I realized that we were now just where we needed to be — outside the old mining town. "All right, gang," I said, "the monster hive is right down there. Let's get the control panel down there and plug it in."

But an ominous voice stopped me in my tracks. At the end of the alley I saw the huge, armored figure of the Black Knight Ghost. "You'll go nowhere, knave!" he thundered as he raised his long, pointed lance.

"Take the long way around," I said to Velma. "I'll hold him off!" Velma looked worried, but she clutched the panel and led the rest of the gang away.

The Black Knight Ghost began approaching me. I had to come up with a plan. Luckily, I'm good at that. I spotted an old pipe lying against a building and yanked it loose. The pipe would be *my* lance.

I jumped on one of the old motorcycles and revved the engine angrily.

The Black Knight Ghost stamped his feet.

I began to move toward my opponent. And then we were off at full speed, each one of us racing toward the other.

Smash! We hit! The impact sent both of us flying into the air. I clutched my side as I hit the ground. The pain was awful.

Bang! Crash! I saw the Black Knight Ghost come down nearby, causing a cloud of dirt to rise around him. The ground even shook when he fell. But — unlike me — he got up right away, unhurt.

With his armor clanking, he began to stomp toward me.

CHAPTER 14

VELMA

I held tight to the control panel as we raced toward the old silver plant and the monster hive. We stumbled down the steep hill that Scooby and Shaggy had fallen from and came to a stream at the bottom of it. "Come on!" I called as I splashed through the water. Scooby and Shaggy crossed it and Daphne was just at the stream's edge when a roar of static filled the air. The stream was suddenly sparking with electricity.

The 10,000 Volt Ghost shot lines of electric current into the water, creating a kind of electric fence. The zapping, crackling fence now separated Daphne from Scooby, Shaggy, and me. "You guys go!" Daphne shouted to us. "I'll take care of Sparky!"

I hated to leave her, but there was nothing we could do for her here and, if we got to the monster hive, we had a better chance of knocking out the monster from there. So we ran on to the old mining town.

We screeched to a stop, though, when we spotted the Pterodactyl Ghost guarding the main street into the town. The big sign hadn't been strong enough to hold it and now it was once again looking for us. Just as it glanced in our direction, I pushed Shaggy and Scooby into a small shack and dove in after them.

I had to think. Fred wasn't here to make a plan, so it was up to me. After a moment, I knew what to do. I handed Shaggy the control panel.

"Like, why are you giving this to me?" he asked.

"I'll distract that prehistoric pinhead. You and Scooby get this to the monster hive," I instructed him.

Shaggy's eyes went wide and he turned pale. "Us?!"

"You're faster than me," I explained. "Once you're there, you just plug it into the base. I fixed it so it will destroy all the monsters."

"But . . . but," he sputtered. "But . . . we can't! We want to be heroes like you, but we're not."

"That's funny," I said. "I always wanted to be like you guys."

Scooby and Shaggy seemed baffled by this, but it was true.

"You're always yourselves, whether you're joyful, or fearful, or hungry. See? Maybe you've been a couple of heroes all along. You just haven't known it."

They seemed happy about what I'd said. Unfortunately, this was no time for a team moment. That Pterodactyl Ghost was sitting out there and, unless I got it to move, Scooby and Shaggy wouldn't be able to get past with the control panel.

Hurrying out of the shack, I picked up a rock I found lying in the alley. The Pterodactyl Ghost had turned away from me, so I had to yell to get its attention. "Hey, Tweety, over here!" I shouted as I hurled the rock with all my strength. I hit it square on the rump. The giant bird monster turned toward me, screeching furiously.

I had a sudden moment of panic, wondering if my plan had been so smart, after all. I dove for the dirt as the Pterodactyl Ghost flew over me. It buzzed the top of my head with its wings when it tried to scoop me up. I rolled out of its path, but it flew back again, preparing for another attack.

I spotted a vent shaft by an old building nearby and jumped into it. "Jinkies!" I shouted as I swirled down and around in the darkness. Then . . . *wham!* I landed hard in a dimly lit room and felt my glasses fly off my face. Where had they gone? I couldn't tell.

Reaching out, I made contact with a cool wall and groped along it. I saw well enough to realize that there were newspaper clippings taped to the wall. And I accidentally flipped some projector switch on the wall. Squinting, I made out a picture of Jonathan Jacobo. There was a picture of him holding the Pterodactyl Ghost costume. I squinted more and saw that the whole room was Jacobo's shrine to himself! There were statues, paintings, pictures everywhere. How I wished I could see better so I could make out exactly what they were. I groped blindly, grabbed one of the photos, and stuck it in my pocket.

"Velma?" came a voice.

I jumped back. Who was there?

Then someone handed me my glasses. "Lose something?"

"Patrick!" I cried as I put the glasses on. At first I was glad to see him. But then I remembered that he was our number one suspect. "What are you doing here?" I asked, trying not to sound frightened.

"Attempting to solve this mystery, just like you," he replied.

I had fallen right into the clutches of the evil mastermind himself. I couldn't let him get me. The fate of Coolsville depended on it.

My talk with Scooby and Shaggy came back to

me. I admired the way they always did what came naturally to them. This seemed like the perfect time to act just the way they did — so I ran away as fast as I could.

I raced out of the room and came to a high, narrow metal catwalk that crossed a large open space. I looked down and couldn't even see the bottom. I heard Patrick running behind me and moved out onto the walkway.

Patrick was getting closer. I had to run faster. But then, with a rumble, the far end of the catwalk became disconnected. *Bang!* With a screech of clanking metal, it dropped, and I slid to the end of it. Just as I was about to plummet into the deep pit below, I managed to grab onto the very end of the catwalk. I dangled in midair, holding on with only one hand.

I could hear that Patrick was still coming after me! He clattered down the tilted catwalk and grabbed hold of my wrist. "Velma, let go," he said.

I wasn't falling for that trick. "Why, so you can drop me and watch me fall to my death?" I cried.

"So I can help you up," he said. "You have to trust me."

"No!" I shouted. "I only trust facts! They're reliable! They don't let you down! And all the facts say you're the Evil Masked Figure."

"But what does your heart say?" he asked.

Clank! The metal catwalk slipped farther.

Patrick knelt and extended his hand out to me. "What does your gut say?"

I didn't know. I wasn't a listen-to-my-gut kind of gal. "No!" I cried as my hand slipped from the metal grate I was holding.

Patrick grabbed me before I could fall and pulled me up to safety. "You okay?" he asked.

Before I could answer, the Pterodactyl Ghost swooped out of nowhere and snatched him.

"Patrick!" I shouted as the giant monster carried him off.

It was horrible and confusing. If Patrick was the Evil Masked Figure, why had he saved me? And why had his own monster carried him off?

Somehow I had to get to the monster hive. Maybe I'd find the answers to my questions there.

CHAPTER 15

DAPHNE

I tried to sound confident and tough as I faced the red, glowing 10,000 Volt Ghost. It chuckled and threw sparks all around, but I couldn't let fear cloud my concentration.

"Taste the pain, Mr. Glow-Ugly Thing!" I shouted, getting into fight position, my hands ready to slice, my legs prepared to kick. I made a quick jab and when I connected — whoooaaaa! What a shock! I flew way high into the air, every inch of my body tingling with electricity!

It was painful, but kind of a good thing, too — because when I came down, I landed right next to Fred. But when I looked up, the Black Knight Ghost was standing right over us with a shiny, bumpy ball on a chain that he was swinging in a circle. He was about to clobber us both.

I caught a glimpse of my reflection in the metal weapon and shuddered at what I saw. I looked terrible! My hair was all frizzed from the electric shock and my skin had been burned bright red. But there was nothing I could do about it. I was miles away from my brush and makeup bag now.

"So . . . I guess it's good-bye, Freddy," I said. There didn't seem to be any way we could possibly escape. "I can't believe this is the way I look the last time you'll ever see me . . . with all my flaws showing."

Fred gazed at me lovingly. "You're still the most beautiful girl in Coolsville to me," he said, "because I see what you're like on the inside."

I was so touched. I had always hoped Fred appreciated the real me, but I was secretly afraid he just loved my good looks. Now I knew he truly loved me for who I am.

The Black Knight Ghost roared angrily at us, still twirling his metal ball.

Fred scowled at him. "Can't you see we're talking?" he asked, annoyed at being interrupted.

"Talking is for wimps," the Black Knight Ghost rumbled.

I was surprised to see tears come to Fred's eyes. I had *never* seen him cry before.

The Black Knight Ghost seemed surprised, too. "What are you doing?" he demanded.

"You're not fooling me with that macho front you're putting up," Fred spoke to the monster.

"It's all just a way to cover up your own inability to connect on an intimate level, a way to pretend it doesn't hurt when the evil masked jerk insults you and orders you around. You're like me in a lot of ways. Gosh, it's incredibly sad."

My heart went out to my poor Freddy. I didn't know he had such a sensitive side. How could I, when he never showed it?

The Black Knight Ghost seemed to understand what Fred was feeling because he burst into tears. "It's so true," he agreed through his sobs. Fred stood and held the weeping monster in his arms, patting him on his massive, armored back. "This is the first time in my life anyone has seen me be vulnerable," the ghost sniffed.

It was nice while it lasted, but suddenly the Black Knight Ghost turned back into his evil self, saying, "Unfortunately, that means I have to kill you!"

I guess monsters can't let anyone see their softer side. Fred and I jumped back, trying to get away from him. And just when it looked like things couldn't get any worse, they did. The 10,000 Volt Ghost showed up, blocking us on the other side. We were trapped!

I knew we had to find a way to destroy the horrible, glowing monster before it electrocuted all of Coolsville. The Mystery Machine was parked just a few yards away and its back doors were still open. I caught sight of jumper cables lying there, and that gave me an idea. But I had to let Fred know what I was thinking without giving away my plan. "Honey, in this, our last moment, I really want to *connect* with you," I told him.

Fred gave me an odd look. I could see he wasn't getting it. How could I make him realize I wanted to point out that there were jumper cables in the van, jumper cables that could be used to conduct electricity? "Remember when we were young and you wore that *jumper?*" I tried again.

"Me? In a jumper?" he asked, still not understanding.

Okay, this wasn't going to be easy. I had to be more direct. I nodded toward the jumper cables in the toolbox in the back of the van. "We'd watch *cable* together," I continued.

Fred's eyes suddenly widened. He'd gotten it!

And just in time! At that moment the 10,000 Volt Ghost swooped in, swinging its arms and trying to grab us. Fred grabbed one end of the cables and flung the other end to me. He ran to an electric generator near an old building and clipped his end onto it. I raced up to the sparking, zapping 10,000 Volt Ghost and hooked my end onto it.

Currents of electricity ran wildly between the generator and the 10,000 Volt Ghost. A sick look spread across the monster's face as it realized what we'd done.

Then — *WAVOOOM!!*

The 10,000 Volt Ghost exploded, spraying smoking debris everywhere. Fred and I dove for cover in a nearby ventilation shaft.

We swirled around in the long shaft until we fell hard into a dark room. We felt our way along and came out into a room with a long, broken catwalk — and Velma was walking along it.

"Jeepers! Are you two okay?" she cried.

I guess we *did* look pretty banged up, especially me, with my frizzed-out hair. "We'll survive," I answered.

"Coolsville won't if Shaggy and Scooby don't get here soon with the control panel!" Velma cried.

CHAPTER 16

SHAGGY

Scoob and I poked our heads out of the shack. All we could see were shadows — and they all looked like monsters! Things didn't look good. "Think we can make it, dude?" I asked Scooby.

He shook his head, looking bummed. But he was right. I didn't think we could make it, either. "Well, pal, I guess I just, like, want you to know that no matter what anybody else thinks, you've never been stink-tastic to me."

I meant it, and I think Scoob knew that, because his eyes got all watery. "When it comes to being a best pal," I continued, "you've never screwed up."

All Scooby had to say was "Roo, either, Raggy," and I got teary, too. But this crying stuff had to stop! If we were gonna go out, it would be in style — *our* style. I pulled our last Scooby Snack out of my pocket. "Halfsies?" I asked him, and snapped it right down the middle. With a little bit of goodness in our bellies, we were ready to face whatever was outside of the shack.

It didn't take long before we had to face it. We darted out around a corner, and right in front of us was the Miner 49er, breathing fire! He bellowed, "Your butts are MINE! *Mine*, get it? *Mine*."

Normally, I'd think that was sort of funny. But when a gigantic miner is standing over you with a pickax, sometimes you lose your sense of humor.

But it *did* give me an idea. We ran back around the corner, and by the time the Miner 49er caught up with us, Scooby was armed to fight him with some gas of his own — all he had to do was pull on his tail! The gas blew the fire right back in the Miner's face, scorching him.

It looked like we'd escaped, but we'd, like, only made the Miner 49er even angrier. He was all charred, but that didn't stop him. He lifted his pickax over his head, yelling, "Your choice, lads. We can make this easy or hard. Take . . . your . . . PICK!"

At this point, there was only one thing to do. We screamed and ran for it.

We raced around corners, jumped over wheelbarrows, shimmied up drainpipes, and hid in barrels. Finally, I checked over my shoulder and didn't see the Miner 49er. We'd lost him!

"Our years of practice running in fear like lunatics have, like, finally paid off," I said to Scooby. We'd lost them, at least for the moment.

We turned a corner and came to the abandoned silver plant. "The monster's hive is through here," I said. We went inside and, this time, I wasn't taking any chances. Scooby and I bolted and double-chained about sixteen locks on the door. Satisfied that we were safe, I turned — and faced the Cotton Candy Glob.

The Cotton Candy Glob was easily twenty feet tall, even without the enormous striped paper cone on its head. "You should never have locked those locks," it said with an evil laugh. Scooby and I began to shake and shiver. More than that — we actually began crying. This guy was really scary. "Now you're stuck in here with me, the Cotton Candy Glob!" it shouted.

Scooby and I stopped crying and looked at each other. We had almost forgotten that it was made of *cotton candy*. Scooby licked his lips. I couldn't remember when we'd eaten last, besides that half Scooby Snack. And I mean, we usually eat a whole box each! Cotton candy sounded like just the thing to fill that hungry spot in my belly.

"Man, I think *you're* stuck in here with *us,*" I told it.

We finished that Cotton Candy Glob in minutes. Our bellies were, like, so big, stuffed full of cotton candy! There was nothing left of that creep but its striped cone hat!

"Finally, a monster we could sink our teeth into," I said. After a few extremely satisfying burps, we jumped into the elevator and hightailed it down to the monster hive.

We were greeted by Fred, Daphne, and Velma. They all looked like they'd had a tough time of it. Fred took the control panel out of my hands. "Come on," he said. "We have to put this in place before —"

He stopped talking because the place was suddenly crawling with monsters! They tumbled down the elevator and crept along the broken catwalk.

"— before that happens," Fred finished.

The Evil Masked Figure appeared on the catwalk. "Destroy them, my pets," he ranted. "Don't let the fools put the panel back in its base!"

"Keep away!" Fred yelled as the Tar Monster slithered around his feet, trapping him on the spot. He flung the control panel to Daphne. She had to hurdle over the Zombie to catch it, but just as she got it in her hand, the Tar Monster wrapped around her legs, too! In a split second, she threw it to Velma. But, like, luck wasn't on our side, because Velma jumped to catch it and landed right in another puddle of gooey black tar. She had just enough time to fling the control panel to me before all three of them were totally covered in tar.

"They can't breathe!" I shouted. And there was nothing I could do, because I looked down and saw the same goopy stuff creeping up my legs, too!

The Evil Masked Figure cackled behind me. "Soon your friends will be dead, and Coolsville — destroyed! My revenge will be final. And there's NOTHING you can do about it!"

He was right. There was nothing we could do — we were totally helpless.

Just then, Scooby tiptoed up to me, pointing a huge fire extinguisher at my face. What was going on? "Dude?" I asked.

Before I knew it, Scoob had sprayed me with the extinguisher, and the tar had frozen, cracked, and shattered! I couldn't help smiling. "Like, frostbite never felt so good!" That Scooby was one good friend.

The Evil Masked Figure wasn't worried, though. "You still can't get past my creatures!" He laughed.

I was tired of this guy making all the rules. I turned to look right at him. "Oh, yeah? Go long, Scoob!" I shouted, passing the control panel to my pal.

Scooby had to leap over a pack of monsters, flip in the air, and grab the panel with his paws. He almost got snapped up by the Pterodactyl Ghost, but instead escaped just in time and the Pterodactyl Ghost collided with the sticky Tar Monster. Scoob landed right at the Evil Masked Figure's monster-making machine.

"No!" the Evil Masked Figure screamed in rage. "You're just some stupid dog! You can't do this to me! Who do you think you are?"

"Scooby! Dooby! Doo!" Scoob shouted triumphantly. He slapped the control panel into place. Instantly the machine started to spark, thanks to the changes Velma had made in its wiring.

All around us the monsters started turning into ooze. They dropped in globs on the floor. Fred, Velma, and Daphne were instantly freed.

"Nooooo!" the Evil Masked Figure shrieked.

I smiled at Scooby. We'd done it! And we'd done it *our* way. Maybe we weren't such screwups after all.

CHAPTER 17

VELMA

By the time we walked out of the old silver plant, it was dawn. The place was already surrounded by reporters and camera crews. The police had come when we called them and now they dragged the Evil Masked Figure out into the daylight.

Reporters crowded around sticking microphones in our faces, eager to hear our story. "Mystery, Inc.," a reporter asked, "do you know the identity of the Evil Masked Figure?"

"Well," I replied, "if my hunch is correct, the Evil Masked Figure is . . ."

Daphne ripped off the Evil Masked Figure's mask. "It's Heather Jasper-Howe!" she announced. "She used the green-screen special camera effect to put her image on top of film of the Evil Masked Figure. That way she could make it appear that they were in the same place at the same time."

As Daphne spoke, I noticed Patrick in the crowd. He was safe!

"Heather Jasper-Howe was at the museum when the Evil Masked Figure was on the roof," another reporter pointed out. "How did she do that?"

Daphne nodded and spoke directly to Heather Jasper-Howe. "You almost had me going there, didn't you? You couldn't have done it without the clever help of Ned, your cameraman! He posed as the Evil Masked Figure that night." She pointed to Ned, who stood in the crowd. The police immediately rushed in and handcuffed him.

"But why did she do it?" a reporter asked.

I stepped closer to Heather Jasper-Howe and reached over to the back of her neck. "Because Heather Jasper-Howe is really Dr. Jonathan Jacobo, the original Pterodactyl Ghost!" I announced, ripping off the Heather Jasper-Howe mask.

"How'd you know that?" a reporter asked, shocked.

I pulled out the picture of Jacobo I'd found in his shrine. It had turned out to be just the clue we needed! "This is a picture of Jacobo in front of the Coolsonian. I found it in the shrine that the egomaniac built to *himself.* They didn't even start construction on the museum until two years ago — nearly a year after Jacobo disappeared!"

Shaggy chimed in, helping me explain. "So Jacobo survived that fall off the prison wall. He, like, came back to Coolsville and started his monsteraceous scheme of revenge."

Fred took the picture from Shaggy and held it up. "He adopted the false Heather Jasper-Howe persona so he could turn the media against us," he revealed.

"He framed Wickles by putting the book and the Black Knight Ghost in his mansion," Daphne added.

"And I would have gotten away with it if it weren't for you meddling punks and your dumb dog," Jacobo shouted as the Coolsville police dragged him away, along with Ned.

Shaggy grinned at the TV cameras. "And that wraps up another mystery," he told them.

The film crews and reporters went off to turn in their stories. The gang and I headed to the Mystery Machine.

Patrick caught up to me and drew me aside. "Velma, I know it looks suspicious, me escaping from the Pterodactyl Ghost, but it's because, well —"

"I trust you," I said.

He smiled at me, pleased.

"Patrick, I want to tell you something," I went on. I paused and took a deep breath. This was going to be a little embarrassing, but I had to be honest. "I'm actually not very glamorous or mysterious. But one thing that's true is . . . I like you very much and I'd like to go out with you . . . but this time I'd go as myself."

"I would love that," Patrick said, smiling even wider. "More than anything."

I noticed that the gang had been stopped by a few photographers who were snapping some final pictures of them, so Patrick and I went to join them.

Fred gave Daphne a big kiss right in front of everyone. "I've realized that showing my feelings doesn't make me any less manly. As long as I don't take it too far and *cry*, or something stupid."

Daphne just looked at him. "But Fred, you cried back there with the Black Knight Ghost."

"No," he said right away. "That was . . . face squishing . . . feeling."

I had to smile. They were both smiling, too, until Fred pushed Daphne's hair back from her ears, just as one of the photographers snapped a shot.

"What are you doing?" Daphne asked, looking alarmed.

Fred grinned. "Nothing. Just thought you might want to show your ears a little. I've always loved your little earlobes."

Daphne looked like she was going to cry. She kept her hair back while the photographers took the rest of the pictures.

Scooby and Shaggy posed together, grinning.

A reporter handed Captain Cutler Ghost's mask to Shaggy and asked him to pose in it. Shaggy slipped on the mask, but when Scooby turned and saw him, he panicked. Scooby let out a scream, picked up a microphone, and started whacking Shaggy over the head with it. It took a few minutes before they sorted the whole thing out, but they ended up laughing about it. The two of them really had the right attitude about everything.

Old Man Wickles showed up and spoke to me. "Those two kids used to be a couple of Pickleaculas until I set 'em on the right track!" he said proudly.

Looking around, I saw that Old Man Wickles wasn't alone. Aggie Wilkins, C. L. Magnus, the tattooed guy, and other bad-guy types surrounded us. For a moment, I felt nervous, but then they all started to clap for us.

Fred turned on the Mystery Machine's radio and music filled the air. Everyone felt so good that we all began to dance. Mystery, Inc. had done it again!

"Rooby-dooby-doo!" Scooby cried.